ENEMY ARROWS

Ruff hurried over to his saddlebags. He returned with the feathers he had taken from the lances. He also had one of the arrows he'd pulled from the dog. . . .

"Kiowa," Buffalo Killer pronounced.

"Kiowa?" Ruff was caught off guard. "This far south?"

"Kiowa!"

"I wish to return the boy to his own people," Ruff persisted stubbornly. "If you help me get him back, I will give you the tall horse in return."

"Ruff!"

Ruff ignored his sister. "I ask only to be allowed to take my people to Austin and then I will return and we will hunt for the boy."

"Maybe dead."

"Maybe."

"Maybe never find Kiowa."

"Maybe." Ruff squared his shoulders. "Kiowa are your traditional enemies, true?"

Buffalo Killer nodded impassively.

"Then I will help you hunt and kill them."

*   *   *

SPECIAL PREVIEW!

Turn to the back of this book for a special excerpt from the _____ Western by Giles Tippette . . .

Dea

... The riviting _____ gest gamble, by _____ Western.

Books in THE HORSEMEN Series
by Gary McCarthy

THE HORSEMEN
CHEROKEE LIGHTHORSE
TEXAS MUSTANGERS

TEXAS MUSTANGERS

GARY McCARTHY

DIAMOND BOOKS, NEW YORK

This book is a Diamond original
edition, and has never been
previously published.

TEXAS MUSTANGERS

A Diamond Book / published by arrangement with the author

PRINTING HISTORY
Diamond edition / February 1993

ISBN: 1-55773-857-2

Diamond Books are published by The Berkley Publishing
Group, 200 Madison Avenue, New York, New York 10016.
The name "DIAMOND" and its logo are trademarks
belonging to Charter Communications, Inc.

PRINTED IN THE UNITED STATES OF AMERICA

10 9 8 7 6 5 4 3 2 1

ONE

Rufus "Ruff" Ballou saw the ears of his four-year-old Thoroughbred stallion snap forward and he felt the slightest hitch in the animal's running stride. Ruff drew High Fire in sharply, hand flashing to the worn butt of his Army Colt. Beside him, his older brother, Houston, along with his sister and the Cherokee girl that Ruff loved also reined in their Thoroughbreds.

"What's wrong?" Houston demanded.

"I don't know," Ruff said. "But look at High Fire's ears. He senses something on the other side of that hill."

Houston allowed himself a grin. At twenty-two, he was strikingly handsome and he knew it. "Hell, Ruff! That stallion knows we're almost home. That's all he's lookin' for."

Ruff wasn't convinced. They had just returned from a bloody vendetta into Kansas and there should have been safety and peace awaiting them in the Oklahoma Indian Territory, but Ruff knew better than to dismiss the alert senses of a horse—any horse.

Besides, a vindictive federal judge in Fort Gibson, Arkansas, had placed a bounty on their heads. They were wanted even more by Southerners who mistakenly believed that the Ballous had betrayed the South before fleeing Tennessee in the face of General William Tecumseh Sherman's plundering Union army.

"There shouldn't be *anything* left alive at our homestead," Ruff argued. "When we left for Kansas it was on fire and there was *nothing* left."

"It's just your nerves," Houston said. "You've got the jitters, that's all."

But fifteen-year-old Dixie was not so sure. "What *do* you think, Ruff?"

Ruff watched the way the afternoon breeze played with his stallion's red mane, coming from the south over the hill into their faces.

"All I smell is smoke," Houston said, his voice a little impatient because they'd been riding hard all night.

Ruff dismounted and handed his reins to Dixie. "I'm going to take a hike up this hill and sneak a look down into our valley. High Fire senses something alive over yonder. Might be another horse. Might be bounty hunters waiting for us to blunder into their trap."

Houston's head dipped in reluctant agreement. He dismounted heavily, then pulled his Spencer repeating rifle from his saddle scabbard. "All right, let's play it your way, just in case."

The two horsemen strode up the grassy knoll, leaving the pair of young women to hold their stallions. Overhead, a red-tailed hawk soared on the hot summer updrafts, searching for prey. Far, far to the west, thunder rumbled and lightning flicked like snake tongues from the dirty underbellies of storm clouds. A summer tempest born of the distant Rocky Mountains was blowing into the Indian Territory. The hawk squalled and fled east.

As the horsemen neared the crown of the hill, Ruff removed his hat and Houston saw fit to do the same. They both flattened and then crawled slowly up until they parted the dry grass and peered down at what remained of their homestead.

Ruff's black eyes took in the charred rubble of their cabin, the outbuildings, and the black, skeletal remains of their fences. He clenched his teeth in fury, thinking about all the long, punishing hours he and his Cherokee friends had spent building this homestead up with the idea of it becoming a great Thoroughbred ranch. Maybe this lonesome valley would never equal the lush Tennessee bluegrass country they'd lost to the plundering armies of the North, but it was an idyllic setting bordered by Blackjack oak, sycamore and pine.

"I don't see anything," Houston whispered, "do you?"

"Not yet."

Houston retreated a few feet and rolled lazily onto his back. He stared up at the huge armada of cumulus clouds being chased eastward by the approaching storm. The air was warm and humid, a typical August day in northeastern Oklahoma. Houston removed his bandanna and mopped his brow. "How long is this going to take?"

"A while."

Houston closed his eyes with a sigh. "You are the most suspicious of men," he muttered. "Wake me when it's time to ride."

Ruff ignored his brother's dry sarcasm and turned to watch their Thoroughbreds. Not only were High Fire's ears still pricked forward but so too were the other horses', even those of their eighteen-year-old foundation sire, High Man. No doubt about it, their horses sensed something alive over this hill, and before Ruff was prepared to go forward, he was going to find out what it was no matter how long that took.

A quarter hour passed. Houston began to snore and down below, the horses had stopped paying attention to whatever they'd sensed up ahead. Ruff saw Dixie and Thia sitting on the grass looking bored and wilted. Ruff's sleep-starved eyes burned into the glare of the afternoon sun. Sweat trickled along his spine and leaked from his armpits down his lean barrel to soak into his waistband. Still, he waited motionless, attention riveted to the valley below. Waiting for . . . what?

"Ruff?"

He turned to see Thia inching up beside him. She laid her slim brown hand on Ruff's neck and then brushed his missing earlobe with her fingertips.

"Does it ever hurt?"

"The missing part of my ear?"

She laughed softly. "Yeah."

"No, it just looks bad."

"Not to me. And how many other girls can boast of having a beau with a bullet hole through his earlobe?"

"Not many, I guess," he said, not wishing to be distracted.

"Are we going to rebuild?" Thia asked, pressing her soft body against his long, hard one. "I think we should rebuild. In fact, I'd like to rebuild right here on this knoll."

"Why?"

"Because from here we can enjoy the cool summer breezes and view this whole valley. To me, it's the most beautiful one in the whole wide world."

"Look at it again," he said, eyes focusing on the charred buildings and fences. "It's been defiled."

Thia inched up to lie cheek to cheek with Ruff. She absently brushed her long black hair from her eyes and stared down at the burned ruins of their horse ranch. Ruff heard her take a deep breath and say, "It'll take some time, but we can rebuild. Can't we?"

"I don't know. Houston and I were talking about that last night. Sometimes a place that has been razed leaves a bitter taste in your mouth that won't fade away. Sometimes it's just better to move on."

"Don't say that!"

Thia cupped his face in her hands. Her dark eyes searched the depths of his soul and after reading it, she whispered, "Rufus Ballou, *this* is where we're going to plant our roots. This is where we're going to be married, have children, and raise famous Thoroughbreds."

Ruff drank Thia's beauty in as if it were the nectar of a wild red roses. She was half-Cherokee, he was a quarter. They were distant cousins but that didn't mean anything. They would be married someday and raise fine horses and children. The only thing was, Ruff wasn't sure anymore it would be in this Oklahoma Indian Territory.

But how to tell Thia this was as yet beyond his ability, for he was not, like Houston, a man with the gift of words.

"What's the matter?" Thia asked, frowning. "Is it the burned logs and timbers that bother you so? Well, then, our Cherokee friends can hitch mules up to wagons and haul them away in less than a week."

She kissed his cracked lips. "We had trouble, but that's past us now. This is our home, Rufus. And right on this very spot, we first made love in the moonlight. Don't you remember?"

He felt his cheeks warm. "Sure I do," he said, not looking at her.

She laughed in his ear and hugged him tightly. "And it's been our love nest all summer. That's why I want to build a new cabin for us right here where we can make love forever."

"Thia," he said, knowing he was blushing, "can't we talk about this later?"

An impish grin creased her lips. "What's the matter, Rufus? Houston is fast asleep."

"It's a damn good thing. If he heard you, he'd become unbearable."

"Am I embarrassing you?"

"Some."

Thia's eyebrows raised in mock surprise. "Men! I'll never understand 'em."

When Ruff made no comment, she turned his face toward her and said, "I never loved anyone before you."

"Me neither."

"And I want you to know that I never will."

"Me neither."

"And," she added, "this *is* our home. So you don't give it up just because those Kansas raiders tried to burn us out."

"They did better than 'try,'" Ruff said. "They burned us to the ground. There isn't so much as a hitch rail standing."

"And those who did it are all dead now," Thia said. "We rode north into Kansas where you and Houston shot them down. They'll never, ever return."

"Their friends and families might."

Thia closed her eyes. "Ruff, there's no place where you won't find killers who will stop at nothing to take what they want and God help you if you try to stop them. We're all just a heartbeat away from death. And until this Civil War is finished, we're safest right here in the Indian Territory."

Ruff started to respond but a distant sound sat him bolt upright. "Thia, did you hear that!"

"Yes, but . . ."

They heard it a second time, the unmistakable sound of a horse whinnying somewhere beyond their valley. Ruff frantically crabbed backward, kicking Houston awake. "The horses!" he cried, jumping to his feet and tearing down the hillside.

Dixie had already clamped her hand over High Fire's

muzzle but there was nothing she could do about High Man, and the older stallion, even with his diminished senses, was almost sure to bugle back a response. Ruff saw the old horse lift his head and they all heard another distant whinny. Ruff waved his arms and the stallion momentarily forgot to bugle. High Man stared at Ruff as if he were an apparition. It gave Ruff enough time to reach the old boy and clamp his hand on the stallion's muzzle. Houston and Thia arrived moments later to prevent the mares from whinnying. The Ballous spoke softly to their Thoroughbreds until they were calm. Then Ruff unsnapped a Confederate-issue single-shot Enfield rifle from his saddle ring. He checked the load even though he knew the weapon was primed and ready to fire like the Army Colt resting against his hip. "Houston, are you ready?"

Houston nodded. "But I want the girls to stay here with the horses until we learn who's planning our homecoming surprise."

Dixie's lips formed a protest but Ruff cut it off by saying, "Houston is right. If we stir up more trouble than we can handle, we'll all head for Tahlequah and get help from the Lighthorse."

Ruff and Houston trotted off, circling into the heavier forests off to the east. Forests that would conceal their movement until they were very close to the charred remains of their homestead.

It took them almost an hour to get into position. Ruff knelt behind a tree beside his brother. "I count five," he whispered. "How about you?"

"The same."

"Recognize any of them?"

"No."

Ruff took a deep breath. Two against five were not odds to his liking but if their first shots dropped a pair, then it would even things considerably. "How do you want to do this, Captain?"

Houston was a captain in the Cherokee Lighthorse. "We separate and circle around behind and get the drop on them. I'll give 'em a chance to throw up their hands. If they don't . . ."

Houston didn't finish and Ruff didn't need to ask what would happen if the five ambushers refused Houston's command.

"Luck," Houston said, gripping his repeating rifle and fading away to his left.

Ruff circled to his right. He and Houston had been raised near the Great Smoky Mountains and they'd stalked and hunted wild game since they were old enough to carry a Kentucky rifle. Ruff skirted the concealed men and horses. He couldn't be sure of their purpose, but the odds were that they wanted Ballou hides for the bounties they'd bring over in Fort Gibson.

With his heart hammering in his chest, Ruff finally came to an ideal vantage point and stretched out full length in thickets. Houston was nowhere to be seen but Ruff knew his brother would also be settling into a good firing position.

Ruff studied the men through the leaves. They weren't Cherokee because they were drinking whiskey and several were very light complected. Ruff guessed that they were indeed bounty hunters. All five were heavily armed and they'd obviously been waiting for several days. Ruff could not make sense of their muted conversation.

"Come on, Houston" he breathed, "let's get this over with."

As if hearing him, Houston stepped out from behind an oak tree and threw his rifle to his shoulder. "Hands up!"

Ruff could not see his brother clearly but when Houston's

rifle boomed, Ruff saw a man flip over backward, thrashing in the dead leaves.

Ruff fired his Enfield from ground level. His first target crumpled to his knees, hands batting at his perforated chest as if he were being stung by hornets. Ruff pitched the single-shot rifle aside and drew his six-gun. Men were shouting and firing, and when Ruff fired again, they scattered. One man, gut-shot and bent over double, came staggering toward Ruff, gun blazing in his fist. His face was contorted with rage and as he advanced he sprayed bullets until Ruff drilled him through the forehead.

Two other men reached their horses but Houston charged after them, rifle belching smoke and lead. A horse reared and its rider was thrown into brush. When he tried to come to his feet, Houston shot him twice. The other man was a skilled horseman and he sailed over a fallen log and went galloping north on a thick-bodied buckskin.

"He's heading straight for Thia and Dixie!" Ruff shouted, jumping to his feet and bursting out of the trees to sprint through the ashes of their charred homestead. Behind him, Houston yelled something but Ruff didn't stop. His long legs were pistoning up and down as he crossed the wide valley. The fleeing ambusher topped the hillock and disappeared.

"Dixie!" he bellowed, firing a warning shot into the sky. "Thia!"

Ruff's lungs were on fire as he churned madly up the hill. "Dixie!" he gasped. "Thia!"

When he finally staggered over the crown of the hill, Ruff staggered and cried, "No!"

Thia was down. Their Thoroughbred horses were scattering and the man on the buckskin was trying without success to overtake and catch up High Fire's reins. Dixie was kneeling and firing but the rider was already well beyond pistol range. Ruff charged headlong down the hill, screaming like a crazed demon.

"Thia!" He dropped to her side.

"She's dead, Ruff!" Dixie cried, still trying to fire her empty gun at the retreating horseman. "He shot her down like she was an animal!"

A howl exploded from Ruff's mouth. The rider was a half mile away and in no danger of being hit but when he heard Ruff's cry of anguish, then twisted around and saw him trying to catch High Man, the killer ran for his life.

Ruff had enough presence of mind to walk slowly toward old High Man, who was snorty and acting as if he might bolt and gallop away in fear.

"Easy," Ruff choked. "Easy."

The stallion shivered but recognized its master's voice. Tossing its head and flaxen mane, High Man stood his ground. Ruff collected the stallion's reins and vaulted into his saddle to send the old Thoroughbred racing after the man on the buckskin.

When Thia's killer saw Ruff coming he began to flog his mount. "Yahhh!" he bellowed hoarsely.

High Man could still run like a horse half his age. The old stallion stretched its neck out like a Canadian goose on the wing and devoured the earth.

It was no race. In less than a mile, Ruff had halved the distance and was closing fast. While the buckskin was willing, it wasn't able. Ruff raised his pistol and fired at fifty yards. He missed and jammed his pistol into his holster.

"Goddamn you!" he cried, tears streaming down his cheeks.

The man twisted around in the saddle. He was bearded and dirty. He had a spare pistol and he tried to shoot but accuracy was impossible when you were corkscrewed around on the back of a rough-riding horse.

Ruff drew his bowie knife and leaned over High Man's withers, willing the Thoroughbred forward with its every magnificent stride.

"No!" the killer cried, firing until his pistol was empty and then hurling his weapon away. "Please, no!"

High Man, ears flat, overtook the failing buckskin and Ruff's long arm swept out to drive the steel of his knife into the murderer's kidney. Ruff yanked the blade forward under the ribs and out the man's belly. The rider lifted in his saddle, head back and mouth distended as if shouting a plea at heaven.

Ruff reined his thundering horse off and wiped his bloody blade on his pants legs. He saw the dying man clutching his saddle horn with both fists, collapsing as the buckskin broke into a jarring trot. When the animal stopped, the man rolled forward and landed on his head. His neck cracked like a branch and the buckskin snorted and bolted away in fear. It stopped a few yards distant, lowered its head, and sucked for wind, flanks wetly heaving.

Ruff spun High Man around and sent the old Thoroughbred galloping back to Thia. She really was dead. He dropped to her side and cradled her, wishing that this was just a nightmare. That they'd all awaken to a gentler reality. Ruff began to rock back and forth with anguish.

They buried Thia Eldee Starr by moonlight, deep on the crown of the hill overlooking the valley where she'd wanted to live. They left no cross to mark her grave but Ruff left his heart and took as a reminder a small gold locket and chain. The onrushing storm hit them just after midnight. Lightning shivered brilliantly across the sky, jagged forks stabbing the hilltops. Ruff asked Dixie and Houston to lead the horses down into the trees and he allowed the wind and the rain to wash away his tears.

With dawn, the summer tempest rolled on, leaving a brilliant sunset in its wake. Melon and gold, lavender and magenta, magnificence and splendor. Ruff watched and described it all to Thia in his simple manner of a last farewell. When the sun dried his clothes and floated beyond the eastern forests, he stood and waited until Houston and Dixie brought him their horses.

"What are you going to do now?" Dixie asked.

Ruff leaned his forehead up against wet leather, inhaled its good, familiar scent, and whispered, "I can't stay here, Dixie. Not now I can't."

She hugged him tightly. "I can't, either. Not anymore."

"Same for me," Houston announced. "I'm riding north to find Molly O'Day."

Ruff took a deep, steadying breath. "If you don't wait until the war is over, you'll be caught and executed."

"Don't matter."

Ruff turned and looked at his brother. Houston's face was haggard and drawn. "It matters to Dixie and me."

"Thanks," Houston said. "But I've got to go anyway. Seeing what happened here with Thia made me realize that when a man is in love, nothing else counts. I've *got* to find out if Molly is still alive. If she is, I'll rejoin you and Dixie when the war is over."

Ruff's face turned South. "I'm Texas bound."

"Me too," Dixie said in a small voice.

Far off, Ruff heard the lonesome howl of a coyote. He shivered and raked his sleeve across his eyes before he jammed his boot in his stirrup.

"Mount up, Dixie."

Houston looked up at him. "The horses. They're yours."

"They don't mean much to me right now."

Houston's hand clamped down hard on Ruff's leg. "They're *all* that should matter to you now. They're what our father lived and died for until this damned Civil War killed most of us off. Now, you take these two stallions and mares, and you had goddamn well be ready to die for 'em until we meet again!"

"What'll you ride north if we take all the Thoroughbreds?"

Houston waved his hand absently. "That stumpy old buckskin wandered in a while ago. He'll carry me to Washington. At least on him I'll attract no attention."

"He's slower than a milk cow."

"I'm through runnin'," Houston replied in a cold, gravelly voice.

Dixie hugged her oldest brother. She was only fourteen, but already tall and her face was streaked with tears. "Houston, I love you. I never showed or said it before, but I do."

He squeezed her, then threw her into High Man's saddle. "Now, git on down to Texas, the both of you," he said in a voice that cracked badly.

Ruff let High Fire follow his daddy and the Ballou mares. He guessed he was going to Texas but right now, he was in hell.

TWO

Ruff did not remember much about the next day, and Dixie said very little to him until they arrived at a Cherokee settlement called Saugus, where Dixie found a barn for their exhausted horses. It only took a few inquiries to also locate a room for the night in the home of an old full-blood Cherokee woman whose husband and sons had gone to war for the Confederacy under General Stand Watie.

"They were all killed," the old woman lamented at the dinner table that night. "All dead now. No one to take care of me except myself."

"I'm sorry," Dixie said with sympathy, "but at least you have a good home in a nice village. I'm sure that the Cherokee people will take care of you."

The old woman nodded but she didn't look very optimistic. "This war has broken our people. Some fight for the South, some the North. Who did he fight for?"

Ruff had not said a word. He hadn't even reached for his knife or fork, although they had not eaten in the past twenty-four hours.

Dixie picked up Ruff's utensils and placed them in his hands. "You have to eat," she whispered.

"Why?"

"Because, if for no other reason, Thia would want you to. And Mrs. Lossiah has made us a fine Cherokee meal.

It looks wonderful, what are we eating tonight?"

The old woman was only too happy to explain. "This is yellow-jacket soup. Very good. You like."

Dixie's eyebrows raised. She leaned forward to stare at the contents of the bowl. "Those little dark things in the soup are really yellow jackets?"

"Oh yes. You catch them very early in the morning when they are cold and asleep, then you bake them until brown. After that, you add water, some hominy, grease, and a little salt. But not too much."

Dixie glanced sideways at Ruff, who was lost in misery and paying the food no attention. Hoping to rouse his interest, she pointed to a bowl of steaming meat she thought might be rabbit. "This smells good, what is it?"

"Nice fat groundhog. Taste like coon or cat. I cook just right. Eat plenty."

Dixie forced a smile. "And this?"

"Mush."

"What kind?" Dixie asked timidly.

"Walnut and corn, with a little cabbage and pepper."

"Now, that does sound good!" Dixie helped herself. "And the bread?"

"Bean bread."

Dixie cut a slice, buttered it and chewed. "Delicious! But it tastes more like corn than beans."

"Some corn, too," the old Cherokee full-blood admitted.

"And is that pudding for dessert?"

The old woman nodded. "Blood pudding. You like."

Dixie choked on her bean bread. "I . . . hope we're not too full for desert, but we might be."

The Cherokee woman shrugged. Her skin was beetle brown, her movements quick and birdlike. Her chin was pointy because she had no teeth and her eyes were obsidian, piercing as arrowheads. She directed a bent forefinger at

Ruff. "What's the matter with him?"

"The girl he was going to marry was gunned down yesterday."

"By Cherokee?"

"No," Dixie said, "by whites from Kansas."

"Why they kill her?"

Dixie didn't want to talk about it to this woman and yet, she had no wish to offend her, either. "It's a long story."

The old lady shrugged her narrow shoulders. "We have a long time. Nothing else to do tonight, huh?"

"Maybe later."

Ruff looked up from his plate. He was sitting at one end of the table, the old woman at the other. "Her name was Miss Thia Eldee Starr and the man that killed her was bloodthirsty and maybe crazed with fear. It doesn't matter. He shot her down and then I cut him. That's all that counts."

The old woman blinked. "Did you kill this man?"

"Yes."

"Good! I would hunt and then kill the men who killed my husband and sons, but they were just bluecoat soldiers."

"Yeah," Ruff said, "in battle, killing is supposed to be different somehow. But the dead are just as dead."

The woman pointed at Dixie and said, "You eat. Maybe this girl become your new woman."

Ruff exploded in anger. "She's my kid sister, you meddling—"

"Ruff!" Dixie jumped up and threw her arms around her brother. "I never even thought to tell Mrs. Lossiah that I was your sister. She didn't know."

The knife and fork dropped from Ruff's hand. He stared at the woman and then his shoulders drooped. "I apologize.

You see, Miss Thia Starr was my first and only love."

The old Cherokee woman's face softened. "You love again before too long. Even with missing part of ear, some girl, she snap you up pretty damn soon."

Ruff blushed. He pushed back from his chair and excused himself and headed for the door.

"Where are you going?" Dixie wanted to know.

"For a walk."

"We'll save your dinner."

Ruff didn't much care. He knew that he wasn't going to starve to death or do any harm to himself, but beyond that he was making no promises. He wished that gutting the man who'd shot Thia had given him some relief from the sickness he felt inside, but it hadn't. Revenge was a little like making love; it felt hot and sweet, but it might also leave you feeling empty.

He reached into his pocket and found the gold chain and locket Thia had so prized. Last winter she had discovered the beautiful jewelry in the mud of Tahlequah and had been afraid to ever open it in case it held a photograph and she recognized its owner or giver. Now, Ruff finally opened the locket.

It was as empty as he was inside. Ruff snapped the locket shut and walked up into the hills until he came to a fallen log, which he stretched out upon while he contemplated stars shining like midnight diamonds. Trying to bolster his spirits, Ruff struggled to list reasons to be thankful. Instead, he kept thinking of how in less than two years he'd lost his father and three older brothers, all direct casualties of the Civil War. Micha and John had been slaughtered on the infamous battlefields at Bull Run and Shiloh. Mason had died near Missionary Ridge and his father had fallen trying to protect the last of his beloved Thoroughbred horses from being confiscated by a

Confederate patrol needing them to pull supply wagons and heavy artillery.

Ruff didn't know how any fool could have thought that the Ballou Thoroughbreds could be used in harness. They were too high strung and fine boned for pulling heavy wagons. But the foolish cavalry officer had insisted, and when Justin Ballou refused to give up the last of his horses, the captain had reached for his pistol. After the gun smoke had cleared, the captain as well as several of his cavalrymen were dead and the Ballou name was forever cursed in the South.

Ruff dozed and awakened much later feeling badly chilled. He stood up and got his bearings, then moved back down to Saugus. There being no saloons in the Indian Territory, the town was boarded up as quiet as a church and there wasn't a soul on the main street. Ruff trudged back to Mrs. Lossiah's cabin, remembering that he had not been much of a gentleman at her dinner table.

"Where have you been!" Dixie demanded, coming out of a chair on the porch and leaning on the railing. "I've been worried half-sick over you!"

"I'm sorry," he said, feeling guilty. "I dropped off to sleep."

Dixie snorted with anger. "Well I'm glad *someone* got some rest this night because I sure didn't!"

Ruff was almost a foot taller and a hundred pounds heavier than his sister but when Dixie got her back up, she could be a real alligator. "Let's get some sleep."

"I'm not sure that I can sleep now."

"I hope so," Ruff yawned. " 'Cause I sure can."

She doubled up her fist and would have pelted him if he hadn't trapped them in his own callused hands. "I am sorry. I was thinking about Thia, as I'm sure that you guessed, and about Pa, Mason, Micha, and John. And about Wildwood Farm and how it looked in the autumn when the leaves turned bright red and orange."

"They'll turn just as pretty in Texas," Dixie said, the anger washing out of her as fast as it had washed in. "Oh, Ruff! We've both got to look ahead instead of behind. There's been too much killing and heartache."

"I know."

Dixie leaned her head against his chest. "In Texas," she whispered, passionately, "we'll start all over again. We'll find a place to build and raise fast horses."

"Sure we will." Ruff inhaled deeply and let his breath out slow. Overhead, the stars were beginning to die and he realized it was well into the morning. "And before too long, Houston will come galloping into our yard with Molly O'Day at his side. Or maybe she'll be Mrs. Molly Ballou by then."

Dixie looked up at him. "Maybe so."

Ruff slept until midafternoon and when he awoke, he felt refreshed although his heart was still heavy with sadness and his step lacked its usual energetic spring. He dressed and went outside to find Dixie and Mrs. Lossiah sipping hot sassafras tea.

"It's delicious," Dixie said, her lips stained red by the sassafrass. "Aggie has spiced it with molasses. Would you like some?"

Ruff would have preferred strong coffee but he did not wish to offend Mrs. Lossiah any more than he already had over dinner last night. "Sure."

They had tea on the porch while the old Cherokee did most of the talking. She talked about how her people had been driven westward out of Georgia, the Carolinas, and Tennessee.

"It is called by our people the Trail of Tears, and of thirteen thousand who began that walk, more than four thousand died along the way. We come here to live but now the whites want this land, too."

"I know," Ruff said. "My brother Houston rode as a captain with the Cherokee Lighthorse. Because of it, he's got a bounty on his head over in Fort Gibson."

"Is he dead now?"

"No. He went to the North to find the woman he loves."

"He's probably dead then," Aggie said.

Seeing the stricken look on Ruff's already sad features, Dixie said quickly, "Aggie says that there is a mix-blood family of Cherokee leaving for Texas tomorrow. I met the father and he's a wonderful man."

"I'm sure," Ruff said absently.

"And we talked a long time," Dixie said, her eyes shining with excitement. "He's very special and wanted to know if we might be willing to all travel together."

"I don't think so."

"Why?"

"Well," Ruff hedged, sensing that this was quite important to his sister, "it's just that we're traveling light and fast. Just us and our horses. We don't need any family to slow us down with women and children."

"I'm a woman!"

"But you're . . . different," he said quickly. "I mean, you're a *horse*woman. You travel as light and as fast as a man. In fact, you travel even better than most men."

Ruff quickly learned that this crumb of a compliment to appease his sister was wasted. "But the road south into Texas is dangerous! Anyone will tell you that there are lots of raiders and deserters from both armies. If we had this man and his family for company, we'd be much safer."

While this made sense, Ruff still didn't care much for the idea. However, after his unseemly behavior the previous evening, he did not wish to be a boor or to dash his sister's obvious excitement over the plan. Besides, Ruff had also heard that the road down to Texas was frequented by outlaws and cutthroats. And even if he felt no concern for his own welfare, he had to think about the safety of Dixie and the Ballou horses.

"What's this man's name?"

"Tucker. Reverend Moody Tucker."

Ruff stiffened. "A minister?"

"A man of God," Dixie said reverently. "He's a preacher and a publisher of the Word."

"Oh." Ruff wasn't too pleased. If in fact the road south was dangerous, he'd have much preferred a man of the sword to a man of the cloth.

"Reverend Tucker said that he would be honored to accompany us south. He's heading for Austin and hopes that we will do the same."

"Can I think about this?"

"What's to think about?" Dixie wanted to know. "He's a fine Christian man with a fine family who needs our help."

"But I never said anything about going to Austin."

"It's supposed to be an ideal place," Dixie argued. "It's the capital!"

"Yeah, but—"

"Please!"

Ruff relented. "I don't know anything about Texas so I guess one part of it is about as good as another."

Dixie brightened. "Why, that's what I told the reverend you'd say. He informed me that Austin is fertile ground for gaining converts to his church—as well as establishing a great horse ranch."

"Did you tell him we had Thoroughbreds?"

"No, why?"

Ruff sighed. "Because we're raising racehorses and that means they run for money. It's gambling."

"Oh. I hadn't thought about that."

"Well, you should have," Ruff said. "Most preachers consider gambling a high old sin. What kind of a preacher is he? Baptist? Methodist? What?"

"Neither. He calls his denomination the Gospel Fire."

"Oh, Lord," Ruff groaned. "He must be a hellfire-and-brimstone preacher. A Bible-pounding evangelist!"

"He's a man of God," Dixie snapped. "And he along with his family needs help and protection as they spread the Word throughout the wilderness."

"Good heavens, Dixie! How much time have you spent with this man? You already sound like a convert."

"Just because you have very few spiritual leanings," Dixie said, "that doesn't mean that I can't unchain my soul and free my earthy bonds."

"Earth*ly* bonds," Ruff corrected. He jammed his fists into his pockets. "Listen, I think this Reverend Moody Tucker and I might just not get along too well. Now I don't mean to be—"

"*Shhh!*" Dixie clenched her hands together and raised them in supplication. "Don't you see that it was meant to be?"

"What?"

"That a man of the cloth should enter our lives—us needing him—he needing us. It's providence, Ruff!"

"Oh, no! It's a complication," Ruff argued, shaking his head back and forth. "I know what you're thinking—that I'm drowning in sorrow and that this preacher will lay the word of God on me and I'll be healed and made whole again. That's it, isn't it?"

For one of the rare times ever, Ruff had Dixie off balance and she sputtered, "Well, sorta, but . . ."

"Dixie, Dixie," he sighed, "I *will* heal. And probably even love again. I don't need to be quoted from Scripture and lectured by some Cherokee Bible banger. Time, nature, and being around our horses will heal my sorrows."

"Reverend Tucker is only a quarter-blood, like us," Dixie said, face coloring with anger. "And it wouldn't hurt you at all to listen to the word of God on a bended knee once in a while! You and Houston both could stand a little Christian humility."

"That's it," Ruff said, backing up and trying to curb his anger. "I have no quarrel with Reverend Tucker now and I don't want to later. Tell him that we intend to travel alone."

"That's not fair! We need him, he and his lovely family need us."

"I don't need him," Ruff said, starting to turn away.

But Dixie grabbed his arm. "Think about this, Rufus. What if he and his Christian family are set upon by murderers and thieves? And they are killed or defiled!"

Ruff saw the trap for what it was—the old guilt pit. Well, he wasn't stepping into it, not this time. "That's why the reverend should stay here in Saugus."

"But he heard the Lord calling him to Austin! And . . . and he has a sister there whose husband has a thriving mercantile business and who can help them get resettled."

"Ah ha! So that's the reason the reverend is going! Well, I'm sorry," Ruff said, turning and stomping away, "but he'll just have to wait for someone else to escort him and his family to Texas."

"But you need to at least meet him and his family!" Dixie shouted. "At least meet them and tell them you won't be bothered, dammit!"

"You tell 'em," Ruff hollered over his shoulder. "You've probably already told 'em every other damned thing about me."

Dixie screeched like a scalded cat but Ruff paid her no mind. He was rested and so were their horses. The best thing he could do now was to head south pronto, before Dixie, the reverend, or that yackety old Cherokee woman latched on to him for some other damned thing.

THREE

Ruff spent a long time currying the horses and he couldn't help but notice how dull their coats appeared. Their old foundation sire, High Man, appeared especially worn down and even his handsome young son looked peeky. Their two Thoroughbred mares were walking bags of bones. They'd both nursed foals in the spring, foals that Ruff and Dixie had given to the Cherokee who'd helped them to build what they'd expected would be their new home.

"You all need rest," Ruff said, running his hands over High Man's ribs. "You need grain and lots of rest."

"The Lord calleth upon man to observe his Sabbath!" a booming voice proclaimed loudly enough to startle Ruff and his horses. "And today is the Sabbath, praise the Lord!"

Ruff twisted around just in time to see a big, florid-faced fellow with red hair and a huge grin come waddling into the barn followed by a brood of children and a chubby, serene-looking wife.

"Peace of the Lord be with you, Brother!" the Reverend Tucker exclaimed, jabbing a ham-sized hand at Ruff.

"Afternoon," Ruff said, watching his hand disappear into the reverend's paw.

The reverend shook Ruff like an itchy bear might a sapling. Then he stepped back and said, "Your fine young sister—a child of God, a child of God—has told me and the missus a great deal about the sorrows you have known these past few years."

Ruff finally managed to extricate his hand. Reverend Tucker was not the equal of his own height, but still outweighed him by seventy or eighty pounds. He had the girth of a good-sized pony.

"Everyone has suffered because of this war," Ruff said, stepping back and then tipping his hat to Mrs. Tucker and her many children.

"Beautiful, ain't they!" the reverend bellowed, following Ruff's eyes. "Little angels, ever single one."

"They are a handsome family," Ruff agreed, guessing the children ranged from a girl of about fourteen on down to the babe in Mrs. Tucker's arms. "They're real special."

"*All* God's children are special!" The reverend beamed. His wife, a short, round blond with nice Scandinavian features, beamed. "All special, as you are, Mr. Ballou. The Lord tells us we are the chosen."

"Yes, ma'am." Ruff mumbled self-consciously. He'd never had much religion after his mother had died and he felt inadquate as to his knowledge of the Scriptures. To Ruff, God was everywhere, most especially in nature and in the beauty of his most perfect living creation, the horse.

The reverend wore a wide-brimmed black hat, a black suit, and a cleric's starched white collar. He looked like a Jesuit except that he was much more exuberant and, surrounded by his harvest, obviously not a celibate. His suit was worn shiny and his wife's dress was faded and threadbare. But the thing that Ruff became most aware of was that the Reverend Tucker possessed the eyes of a fanatic—black and shiny like his suit. If he had not been a man of the Lord, Ruff would have suspected him of being nerve jangled by something like morphine or laudanum.

The reverend introduced each one of his children: Rebecca, Jonah, Ezekiel, Rachel, right on down to the smiling infant whose name was Matthias. Each child who was old enough stepped forward when introduced, bowed or curtsied, and then chirped, "Glad to meet you, Mr. Ballou!" before offering their hand.

Ruff shook each little hand and when he stared into the trusting blue eyes of a freckle-faced red-haired girl named Monica, he knew that he was hooked into leading this family down to Texas. It didn't help any when he saw Dixie grinning at him from the doorway of the barn.

"Now then," the reverend said, voice still so loud it made the horses quake, "about this Texas business. Sir, we'd pay you if we were blessed with coin, but failing that, I hope to repay you far more amply with instruction in the ways of our Lord."

"No payment is expected," Ruff said quickly.

"Ah, but *much* is expected of us, my son! You have your work. Mine is to preach the gospel."

"I understand, but—"

"These are fine horses," Mrs. Tucker said, speaking up for the first time. "Tall but a little thin, aren't they?"

"Yes," Ruff admitted. "We've been on the run since the battle of Missionary Ridge and Lookout Mountain over by Chattanooga, Tennessee. War is hard on beast as well as man."

"War," Tucker snapped, "is an outrage against all of humanity! It is a sacrilege to take life! A sacrilege of the highest order—that is, except to preserve one's *own* life or that of his friends, family, or other innocent members of the flock. Wouldn't you agree, Brother Ballou?"

"I would indeed." Ruff was glad that the reverend wasn't a Quaker or some such group that were totally opposed to all violence. The last thing he wanted was to have this man refuse to bear arms against any attackers they might meet on the road to Texas.

"We have a calling in Austin," Tucker grandly announced. "An urgent calling by God to build a new mission, school, and a Gospel Fire ministry that will chase the devil to hell out of Texas!"

"Well," Ruff said, eyes darting to Dixie for help, "I'm sure you do. But I have to be honest. We have never been to Texas before. So . . ."

"The Lord will guide and the Lord will provide!"

"Amen!" wife and children called.

"Would you care to take supper with us tonight?" the reverend asked. "Mrs. Tucker is preparing some excellent hominy and possum stew."

"No, thank you," Ruff said quickly for he had seen a café on the main street and wanted piles of beef and potatoes drenched in gravy with biscuits and apple pie. Normal, rib-sticking fare that would put a spring back into a man's step.

"And blood pudding," Mrs. Tucker added quickly. "I learned the recipe from Mrs. Lossiah. It is wonderful!"

"I'm sure it is," Ruff said, "but no, thanks, I need to make preparations for tomorrow. However, I know that my sister will be more than happy to join you and your family."

"Delightful!" the Reverend Tucker exclaimed. "We don't have much, but what we do have is enough. The Lord always provides."

From the looks of the Tucker family, Ruff thought that the Lord was indeed bountiful. These were not skinny people and he wondered if they ate out of their own larder or usually feasted at the expense of Tucker's parishoners. Probably the latter, unless the flock was very generous indeed when the collection plate was passed around each Sunday.

"In the morning, then," Reverend Tucker said, stabbing out his huge hand.

"In the morning," Ruff responded, trying not to show pain, for the reverend's grip closed like a bear trap.

When the family had all trooped off, Dixie came over to Ruff and she was furious. "Why did you tell them I wanted to take supper with them!"

"Because," Ruff said, putting away the curry comb and thinking of the steak he would soon be enjoying, "you've gotten me into this business and I thought it only fair that you paid a price for your interference."

"What plans! Since we left our new homestead, we haven't had any plans except some vague idea about going down to Texas. At least now we have a destination and a purpose."

"Which is?"

"To make sure that the Reverend Tucker and his family arrive safely."

"The Lord will see to that," Ruff said.

Dixie's eyes slitted. "Don't you be makin' fun of the faith, Rufus Ballou! I know that you didn't ask for any of this, but now, instead of thinking about how bad you feel over Thia's death, instead you'll start thinking about helping this God-fearing family."

Ruff had to nod his head in agreement. "You're right," he said. "I will."

Mollified, Dixie complained, "I sure don't want possum stew and hominy for supper. And the idea of facing another bowl of blood pudding makes me want to retch."

"Tough it out," Ruff said. "Give it up to God."

Anger flashed in her eyes. "Sometimes you make me want to bat the rest of that bad ear off, Rufus!"

"I'm sorry." He headed for the door. "I'll see you tonight after supper back at Mrs. Lossiah's cabin. We'll get a good night's sleep and then an early start."

Dixie didn't say anything as she followed him outside but her expression was grim.

Ruff awoke early the next morning and the old woman had some warm, delicious-smelling bread on her hearth. Ruff was almost afraid to ask what was in the bread for fear that it might spoil his appetite. He feared that it might include cooked beetles or some such questionable delicacy.

However, his curiosity was so great he could not help himself from asking. "What kind of bread is this?"

"This is an old Cherokee favorite called bean bread," the woman told him. "My Cherokee grandmother taught me how to make it long ago, when we hid from soldiers in a cave on the Tennessee River. I was just a little girl when they found and marched us to the Indian Territory."

"You were on the Trail of Tears?"

"Yes." Aggie swiped at her eyes. "Granny died and so did my mother. But I remembered about this bread and cooked this yesterday while you and your sister were sleeping."

The old woman handed Ruff a slice after splashing it with butter. The bread was dense, dark yellow, and fine textured. When Ruff took a bite, it tasted like excellent corn bread but with a little something extra.

"Do you like it?"

"It's great!"

"I pour a hot bean soup over fresh cornmeal and add wood ashes lye to the meal until it gets real yellow. Then

I work it around in a kettle over the fire and when it gets sticky, I take it out and work it with my hands until it feels smooth. Sometimes I add a little sugar or honey."

"I can taste the honey," he said, devouring the bread and hoping she'd offer him more.

Aggie did. She gave him half a loaf, which must have weighed a full pound. Then she sat down and pleasured herself with watching Ruff eat.

"My husband and sons loved that bean bread," she commented wistfully. "I would make ten loaves all at once and they'd eat them up in two days—if I hid them most of the time."

The old woman's eyes grew misty with memories. "I have no strong men to cook for now."

With his mouth full of the delicious bean bread, Ruff really did not know what to say that might make the old full-blood Cherokee woman feel better, so he kept quiet and let her talk.

"I cooked ten loaves yesterday for you and the Tucker family," Aggie said, pulling herself back into the present. "Those people will eat it all up by themselves if I don't give you a couple of loaves to hide."

"Dixie and me will sure enjoy them." Ruff took a swallow of the steaming tea that she had poured and grinned. "Peppermint tea, right?"

The old lady dipped her pointy chin. I'll tell Dixie where to look for it on the road to Texas. It's good for cold mornings."

Ruff agreed as he enjoyed his breakfast of bean bread and peppermint tea. "You ever been down to Texas?"

"No," Aggie said. "This has been my home since I was married."

"You heard much about Texas?"

Aggie shrugged. "I know there are Cherokee in Texas. The great Sam Houston was our good friend. He died last year."

"So I heard. He was a man that we all admired, even if he was an anti-secessionist. I hear the ungrateful Texans threw him out the governor's mansion because he wouldn't support the Confederacy—never mind that he saved their republic and whipped that bloodythirsty Santa Anna."

"I saw General Houston once," Aggie Lossiah said proudly. "It was in Tennessee and I was just a small girl. He was twice elected as the governor of Tennessee, you know."

"I know. My father voted for him and it broke his heart when Houston left his wife in a scandal and fled to Texas. Father named my brother after Sam Houston and said Houston's wife wasn't worth spit."

"I think maybe Texas needed him more than Tennessee," Aggie said. "I wish he'd have come to Oklahoma instead."

Ruff smiled. He had heard about General Sam Houston and his heroics down in Texas since he was just a boy. The fact that the general had became an ardent anti-secessionist had never diminished the great man in the eyes of Justin Ballou. And, to be frank, one of the primary reasons that Ruff wanted to see Texas was to finally visit the Alamo. It had fallen ten years before Ruff was even born, but it had always seemed very sacred to him and he'd never tired of hearing the story of the 177 brave men who'd died fighting for Texas independence from Mexico back in '36.

Aggie pinched off a hunk of the bean bread, swabbed it generously with butter and said, "What do you think of Reverend Moody Tucker and his family?"

Ruff glanced up, his vision of the Alamo dissolving. "I don't know. The reverend seems like a fine man and I liked his wife and children."

"He's a powerful preacher," Aggie said. "He holds revivals in a tent and saves many souls."

"I'm sure he does."

Aggie winked. "He saved so many souls in the Indian Territory, most of them got lost again so that he could save 'em all over."

Ruff chuckled. "I hear he's got a rich brother-in-law in Austin."

"Ha! Everybody knows that the Reverend Tucker and his Gospel Fire ministry is always short of money."

"He has a large family that seems to enjoy food," Ruff said, being as tactful as possible.

The old woman's eyes dropped to her lap and she pressed her thin lips together in a tight line indicating that she had nothing more to say in this matter.

Ruff's brow furrowed. "Is there something else that I should know about the reverend?"

When the woman didn't answer, Ruff added, "I know that Reverend Tucker is a man of God, but I would also like to think he will not be a burden to me on the way down to Texas. I need to know if he will fight if we are attacked by thieves or killers."

Ruff waited a moment. "Will he fight?"

Aggie Lossiah raised her head. "He will fight," she said in the strangest voice, adding, "Moody Tucker will fight like the devil himself."

"Good!" Ruff finished his bean bread and peppermint tea. "I've got a lot to do this morning before we leave so I'd best get Dixie moving."

Aggie extended her frail, bony hand and Ruff felt a strong affection for the old widow. He sensed that she really wished he and Dixie were staying in Saugus and not going to Texas. He also sensed she knew a great deal more about Reverend Tucker than she'd admit.

Well, Ruff thought as he went out to get their Thorough-breds ready for the long trail south, he would just have to wait and learn all about Reverend Tucker during the journey. One thing that would not be a surprise, Ruff felt quite sure, was that Tucker's wife and children were just as good as gold and sweeter than Mrs. Lossiah's peppermint tea.

FOUR

"Good morning," Dixie called as she entered the livery to help Ruff saddle and bridle their horses. "Did you get some of that wonderful bean bread?"

"You bet," Ruff said. "It was delicious. Have you seen the Tucker family this morning?"

"No, but I didn't expect to. They said last night that we should just bring our horses on by their place as early as we wanted and they'd be waiting to go."

"Good. It must be eight o'clock already and I'd like to get out of here before much longer." Ruff looked up from tightening his cinch and tried to stuff a grin. "By the way, how was the hominy, possum stew, and blood pudding last night? Delicious?"

"Go to hell," Dixie muttered as she grabbed a hoof pick and began cleaning High Fire's hooves.

When they were mounted, Ruff learned that the Reverend Tucker's homestead was about four miles north of Saugus, which meant that it was eight miles farther from Texas. Ruff didn't care although he thought that, had their circumstances been reversed, he would have arranged the meeting in town and saved his traveling partner the extra time and distance.

"Now, Ruff," Dixie said after they'd ridden about three

miles, "I think I ought to warn you about what to expect at the Tucker place."

He glanced sideways at her. "What's that supposed to mean?"

"It's just that you probably expect to find a nice, tidy cabin and some corrals and barns and stuff. You know, a real homestead."

"I wasn't expecting anything."

"Good." Dixie cleared her throat. "Because that's kind of what you'll see. They, uh, live in their revival tent."

"A tent?"

"Yes, it's pretty large, or at least it used to be before it got blown up into the trees during a high wind last winter. Now, the little kids sleep in a wagon and—"

"A wagon?"

"Yes. Nothing wrong with that, is there?"

Ruff scowled. "I'm not sure you or I would have been too happy about living in a tent or a wagon."

"Well," Dixie said, sounding as if she wished she could drop the subject entirely, "the Tucker family seems very happy. The reverend and Anna sleep in the revival tent—or what's left of it—and hold their meetings there when they aren't publishing the *Gospel Fire*."

"They publish?"

"It's a weekly they sell on the streets and wherever else they can spread the Word. The reverend and his wife are very proud of it, front side and back."

Ruff didn't say anything.

"I bought a copy last night. Would you like to see it?" Dixie asked, reaching for her saddlebags.

"Maybe later," Ruff replied. "So what do they have, a printing press or—"

"Exactly! It's kind of old and rusty, but it's a Washington press. Reverend Tucker says that God himself keeps it oiled, inked, and running."

"I hope he helps God a little."

"Actually," Dixie hedged, "the press is sort of broken. That's one of the reasons why the family is moving to Austin. The reverend hopes that his brother-in-law will help him buy a new printing press along with paper and ink. Failing that, they pray he'll at least help them pay for new parts and fix their old press."

It sounded to Ruff as if this family was destitute and desperate. "What about their wagon and team of horses? Are they broken down, too?"

"I saw the wagon," Dixie said, "and it's . . . different. Real unusual."

"*How* unusual?"

Dixie smiled weakly. "Well, it's kind of like a Conestoga only without sides and with a second floor and . . ."

Ruff waited until his patience wore out and then he said, "A what?"

"It's two stories tall."

Ruff groaned.

"They need the second floor," Dixie said. "You know how big the family is. They're planning to load the Washington press on the bottom floor because it's so heavy, then put the kids on top. The children can hardly wait."

"So can I," Ruff growled. "And what happens when we travel through forests? You know there are going to be overhanging tree branches. How tall is this wagon?"

"Pretty tall," Dixie admitted. "At least twenty feet."

"Lord!" Ruff cried. "What kind of a mess have I gotten myself into!"

Dixie's temper flared. "These are awfully good people, Ruff. The salt of the earth. They trust in God and we're just going to have to do the same."

Ruff bit his tongue before he said anything that he might

later come to regret. One thing that his father had always stressed was that once you agreed to do something you had to finish it no matter how galling. And Ruff *had* agreed to help this family reach Austin and he would do so come hell or high water.

"I just want you to know one thing," he told his sister. "If we're attacked and it comes down to the hard choices, I'm going to save you and our horses first."

Dixie's eyes widened with shock. "What about those beautiful children!"

"I care about 'em enough not to rein my horse around right now and leave 'em behind."

Dixie threw him a killer look and then urged High Man into a gallop as she moved up the road leaving Ruff behind to fuss and stew over the way things were going to pieces this morning. Had he been traveling alone, he'd have left hours ago.

"Patience and forbearance," he told himself aloud as he tried to prepare himself for a sight that he knew would soon be no less than appalling.

No amount of preparation could have prepared Ruff for the Tucker homestead. Their tent was collapsed, with children squirming around underneath trying to get out while their mother struggled frantically to free them. The reverend was trying to catch a pair of ugly draft horses that were amazingly fast considering they wore hobbles. But more, much more than all that, was the wagon. It was not to be believed. With monstrous wheels and a treehouse upper story, the thing was a rolling monstrosity. It looked like a double-decked chicken coop and, indeed, the upper deck was wrapped in chicken wire.

"Oh, my God," Ruff breathed, reining in his horse and gaping at the sight. "What have I gotten myself into!"

He would have turned around then, but Dixie grabbed

his arm and said, "Please, we're the only hope they've got of reaching Texas. If we leave them behind, someone will kill them for sure."

Ruff stared at the mess. There were empty and rusting tin cans strewn everywhere and at least one mangy dog for every child—all of them barking, of course. Four or five goats were hopping around on the collapsed tent and a few scrawny roosters were perched overhead in the trees, craning their necks and squawking.

"Courage," Dixie pleaded as she rode forward with Ruff in tow.

By the time they arrived at the tent, Anna Tucker was almost hysterical because her baby was still trapped under the canvas. Ruff jumped down from his horse, grabbed the edge of the canvas, and wormed his way under it while Dixie tried to calm the distraught woman.

The kids were bluish from suffocation by the time they were all extracted from under the huge tent. Anna sobbed her gratitude, hugging Ruff and the children all at the same time.

"Maybe you'd better help the reverend catch up those draft horses," Dixie suggested. "I'll help Mrs. Tucker dig the last of her furniture out from under this tent and get things ready to be loaded."

"I thought they said they'd be ready to leave whenever we arrived," Ruff grated under his breath.

"Well," Dixie hissed, exasperation creeping into her voice, "as you can plainly see, they *aren't*. We'll just have to help them out a little—won't we."

"A little?" Ruff snapped as he strode back to his stallion and mounted. He galloped out to the pasture where Tucker was dashing back and forth, face beet red from his exertions and his corpulent body thoroughly drenched with perspiration.

"Here," Ruff said, pulling his horse to a stop and leaning toward the reverend with his arm outstretched, "give me those halters."

"The devil must be drivin' those contrary sons of . . . guns," the reverend said, catching himself just in time. "I swear that I should have stuck with mules. Had a fine pair once, but I foolishly traded 'em for three weevily bushels of cornmeal, a cream separator, and this pair of worthless nags."

"I'll catch them up," Ruff said, thinking that if he were the draft horses and had any inkling whatsoever that they might have to pull the huge, two-storied wagon, he'd also learn how to run in hobbles.

It took High Fire less than three minutes to chase down both draft horses and bring them to their gasping owner. When Ruff handed the reins to the man, he said, "Are they good pullers?"

"I don't know," the reverend replied. "They're supposed to be."

"You don't know for sure?" Ruff asked in amazement.

"They *look* strong, don't they?"

Ruff dipped his chin, not wanting to say more. A horse could look fast, look strong, look healthy, or any other thing, but their looks were often deceiving. A muscular horse might have weak leg tendons or simply refuse to work. A tall, swift-looking horse might be cursed with bad bones or perhaps have had his wind broken. Furthermore, he might simply look great but run like a milk cow. Looks were worth almost nothing in animals and not much more in people.

"Let's get them hitched to that wagon and then get it loaded," Ruff said. "Time is wasting."

"The Lord gives us the time we need for the things we're supposed to do," Tucker said. "Now, I wonder where the harness went? I saw the children playing with it a few months ago and . . ."

The next four hours were some of the worst that Ruff could ever remember. The harness had been chewed apart in a dozen places by coons, foxes, and the pack of worthless Tucker dogs. Ruff finally got it repaired enough to last but he knew it would have to be replaced long before Texas.

The Washington printing press was a monster to lift and load. It looked like a cannon-riddled water tank and Ruff practically begged the preacher to leave it behind but Tucker refused. The man proved himself as stubborn as he was strong, and they finally got the Washington as well as the furniture and wadded-up tent stuffed onto the bottom floor of the wagon. Over the top of that, they piled trunks and boxes and bags. There was no order to any of it. Everything from stockings to kettles to fishing poles were tossed onto the wagon until there was a pile as tall as Ruff and the stuff on top just kept sliding down the sides and falling off the wagon.

"I guess we'll have to leave the rest behind for the poor folks, bless their hearts," Reverend Tucker said, mopping his brow and hitching up his britches.

Ruff looked at the incredible mass of junk piled on the first floor. "How are you ever going to find anything in there?"

"Oh, the children will sort it out by and by," Anna Tucker said happily. "Give 'em something to do on the way to Austin."

"What about the dogs, goats, and those treetop roosters?" Dixie wanted to know.

"If they come, we'll provide for them, if not, they'll find new homes," Tucker explained.

Ruff fervently hoped they would find new homes, but that proved a futile dream, too, because the older children scrambled up onto the top floor and coaxed the dogs and goats right on after them.

"I'm glad Houston isn't here to see this," Ruff whispered to his sister. "He wouldn't be caught dead traveling with this outfit."

"Let's just hope he isn't dead," Dixie replied.

"Are we ready now!" Ruff called, noting how the sun had passed its zenith and was slipping toward the west.

"Almost," Reverend Tucker shouted, taking his wife's hand and dropping to his knees with a loud grunt. "Children!"

The children let loose of their goats and dogs to also fall to their knees. And given the precariousness of their second-story position, Ruff hoped that they prayed well.

"Dear Lord," Tucker boomed, voice sending roosters sailing back and forth through the treetops, "we are about to undertake a perilous journey. We know that you will protect and guide us with the help of your servants, Rufus and Dixie Ballou. We know, too, Lord, that you will provide us with food and whatever else we require on the way to Texas and that, when we arrive, our dear Brother Roscoe Cudworth will prove himself generous beyond measure. Amen."

Ruff glanced at Dixie and whispered, "I never heard such a prayer."

"*Shhh!*"

Tucker helped his sweet wife up onto their wagon. It didn't even have a seat so they dug a couple of wooden kegs out of the pile and sat on them. "Hee-yaw!"

The draft horses threw themselves into their traces and, for a scary moment, Ruff thought that they weren't going to be able to budge the rolling chicken coop. But the thing finally did break inertia and the Tuckers erupted with triumphant shouts and childish screams of delight.

"Gone to Texas!" Reverend Moody Tucker shouted at

the skinny roosters overhead. "Good-bye, Oklahoma!"

The older kids echoed this refrain all the way back down to Saugus.

It was late afternoon when they arrived and the reverend helped his wife back down from his rolling mountain of trash and slapped his hands together with satisfaction.

"I'd say this was a fine start," he announced to the wide-eyed gawkers that came out to witness the spectacle. "Yes sir, and we're going to have an old-time prayer meeting right here tonight. Mrs. Tucker!"

"Yes, Reverend?"

"Let's get the tent erected and your fiddle warmed up for some good gospel music!"

Ruff blanched. "This is it? This is as far as we go today?"

"The Lord wants me to preach his word one last time in Saugus," Tucker announced. "So, Brother, step down offa that tall horse and please give the Lord and your sister a helping hand!"

Ruff opened his mouth to protest as Tucker marched over to a stump, hopped up onto it, and began to preach to the sky. Dixie almost pulled Ruff out of the saddle, whispering, "Come on! We can't let Anna and the children wrestle that big tent up again."

Ruff was wearing a gun and he had a powerful urge to use it on Reverend Moody Tucker. Already, the crowds that had come to gawk at the wagon were shifting over to hear the reverend preach his usual scorcher. Ruff didn't have time to pay the man any attention because he was too busy dodging flying kids, goats, and dogs while wondering how he was going to keep his sanity on the way down to Austin.

FIVE

The prayer meeting went on until well past midnight and it seemed that almost everyone in town attended. Ruff and Dixie spent another night boarding at Aggie Lossiah's cabin after eating more bean bread, fish soup, and scrumptious apple pie. In the morning, they had a breakfast of pheasant eggs and walnut meal fortified with strips of bacon and washed down with apricot tea.

"That must have been quite an event last night," Dixie said after breakfast. "I could hear them shouting and singing gospels until the wee hours of the morning."

"I slept through it all," Ruff said, anxious to get packed and headed out for Texas.

"The Tuckers might want to sleep in a little this morning," Dixie warned.

"If they aren't loaded and about ready to leave when we get our horses saddled," Ruff began, "I'm for leaving without them."

"Be reasonable. How could they be ready to leave after being up half the night holding a gospel meeting? And them with so many children and animals to care for?"

"Dixie, at the rate we are going, it'll take us the rest of our natural lives to reach Austin, Texas. I'd like to get there still young enough to do something!"

"You will," Dixie vowed. "I was talking to an old man

44

last evening and he says Austin is only about four hundred miles south."

"It might as well be four million if we're traveling with the Tuckers."

Dixie chose not to comment. A few minutes later, they again said good-bye to Mrs. Lossiah and went to saddle their horses. The air was cool and the sky was clear. It was, Ruff thought, a good day for traveling unless you were escorting the Tuckers.

When Ruff and Dixie rode over to the reverend's tent they were surprised to see that the Tucker family had not only finished breakfast, but actually had most of their packing completed. Dixie shot Ruff an accusing glance and he felt guilty enough to dismount and help the reverend and his wife finish loading the tent. It was a patchwork of canvas supported by six long, stout poles and buoyed by heavy rope guidelines. It looked like a military campaign tent that had been shot up and discarded during the Civil War.

"That's exactly what it is," Tucker said, confirming Ruff's suspicions. "It was used by General Robert E. Lee himself at the start of the war. Some folks have even suggested that it's wrong to have a ministry under a tent used to plan battles and destruction, but I say nonsense!"

"I'm sure the Lord would understand," Ruff said. "How did your revival go last night?"

Reverend Tucker grinned. "The Lord came and touched the generous natures of the flock. We are the joyful recipients of almost a hundred dollars for ministerial labors."

"A hundred dollars! That's wonderful!" Ruff said, meaning it because he knew how poor this family was and how badly they would need money on the road south for food, feed, and repairs.

Tucker hugged his wife. "Anna and I are most blessed. Everything we need is given us."

"I'm not telling you what to do," Ruff said, "but you really need four big horses to pull a wagon that size."

"And how much would I have to pay for such animals?"

"A good pair of pulling horses might cost you as much as fifty dollars. And that harness is shot."

The reverend sighed and turned to look at his wife, who said nothing. Finally, Tucker said, "I think we'll just make do with what we have for now. Our larder is pretty low and we're going to have to buy food and supplies along the road to Texas."

Ruff understood. Having only two horses, however, left no room for error or lameness. It also meant that their progress would be much slower. But he was not going to insist that this family buy anything.

"We'll just trust to luck and the Lord," he said.

Tucker beamed. "Exactly, and if—"

"Reverend! Reverend Tucker!"

They all turned around to see a wizened old Cherokee woman come hobbling forward. She was distraught and wailing with grief. Both the reverend and his wife Anna rushed forward. "Dear Mrs. Price, what is wrong!" Reverend Tucker asked, kneeling before her.

"It's Clemson," the woman sobbed, her dark, wrinkled face cut with sharp lines of age and grief. "After he left last night, Clemson said he was feeling closer to God than he'd ever felt in his life. But then, this morning when I woke up, he'd died! He *is* with God now, Reverend Tucker! But he left me alone without children or even enough money for food. And I owe the merchantile store money I can't pay and . . ."

"Poor woman," Anna consoled, wrapping her arms around the old lady. "Mr. Tucker, I think we need to help dear Mrs. Price, don't you?"

"The Lord is bountiful!" Tucker hollered, yanking off his hat and reaching into his pocket. He pulled out a wad of greenbacks and stuffed the whole bunch into his hat, then extended the hat out to the people on the street. "Brethren, God loves the giver. Help us help this poor, suffering sister!"

Almost immediately, people began to step forward to drop money in the reverend's hat. Ruff felt Dixie give him a hard elbow thrust to the ribs. He knew what she wanted.

The preacher had donated every dollar he'd earned last night at the revival without an instant of hesitation. The Ballous could do no less.

"Here," Ruff said, yanking out his own wallet and emptying its contents.

Reverend Moody Tucker grinned, threw back his head, and shouted to the sky, "The Lord will bring you his reward in heaven, brother!"

"I hope so," Ruff said quietly.

Dixie beamed with pride. "That was a fine and Christian thing to do."

Ruff could feel his cheeks burn and while the hat was passed around to the other townfolks who had gathered to say good-bye to the reverend, they all sang, "We Shall Gather at the River." Ruff sang in full voice, though he could not carry a tune in a bucket.

"My brothers and sisters," the reverend announced when the singing ended, "we will have funeral services for Brother Price this afternoon at one o'clock down at the cemetery. Thanks to your generosity, we can have a fine burial and casket and send our dear departed brother, Clemson, off to his Maker in fine style knowing his dear wife will be provided for until she joins him in heaven."

"Amen!" someone called. "Amen!"

"There goes another day," Ruff muttered.

"*Shhh!*" Dixie admonished.

That night at Mrs. Lossiah's they dined on catfish, mushrooms, and cornbread with cinnamon-spiced apples for dessert. The following morning after another large breakfast, Mrs. Lossiah gave them three more loaves of her special bean bread.

Dixie left the woman twenty dollars for her kindness and confided to Ruff, "I guess we've given about all our money away now."

"Yep," Ruff said. "Let's just hope that the Lord will provide because we are dead broke."

"We've some extra guns and holsters we can sell for a fair price," Dixie reminded him.

It was true. They'd kept the weapons from the dead men they'd tracked down and killed up near the Kansas border. Ruff had a half dozen guns and rifles he'd comandeered as sort of a small repayment for the burning out of their homestead by that pack of killers. Those weapons were far better than Confederate cash. Ruff guessed that, altogether, the confiscated weapons were worth a few hundred dollars.

When Ruff and Dixie rode over to the Tuckers' camp, the reverend and his family were all packed and ready to leave.

"Mrs. Price took great comfort in the service yesterday and the money you so generously contributed," Tucker said as he mounted his two-story wagon and grabbed his driving reins.

Ruff swelled a little with pride. "You set the example, Reverend. Now, let's see if we can reach Austin *before* wintertime."

Tucker barked a belly laugh and slapped the lines against his team of horses. The huge chicken house on wheels lurched into motion, the kids screamed and waved good-bye to their friends and all along the street, and the Cherokee citizens of Saugus appeared to wish the Tuckers farewell.

"They were pretty popular, weren't they," Ruff said, a little overwhelmed by the display of emotion he saw as the Tucker family rolled out of the town.

"I told you they were worth waiting for," Dixie said. "Now, we just have to pray that there will be no trouble on the way down to Texas."

"You do the praying," Ruff said. "I'll do the watching."

Dixie looked sideways at her tall brother. "You still haven't seen the light, have you."

"Some things take a little longer than others," Ruff drawled, glancing up at a darkening sky and wondering how many rivers they'd have to ford. And even more to the point, how the two-storied wagon could possibly float or be ferried across deep water.

That question came back to mind a week later, when they arrived at the banks of the Red River. Being late summer, the river was running low but it was still wide, deep, and swift enough that crossing it would be a challenge.

"We can swim it on horseback," Ruff said, studying the red, churning waters, "but I'm not a bit sure about how we can get that top-heavy wagon across."

"Maybe we'll have to hire that big ferry down there."

Ruff twisted in his saddle. He and Dixie were about a half mile ahead of the Tucker's great wagon and they'd both seen the ferry as soon as they'd arrived at the riverbank. The ferry was really just a log raft attached to a steel cable that spanned the river.

"I wonder if that raft is big enough to carry the Tuckers' wagon."

"I expect so," Dixie argued. "It's plenty long and wide enough."

"Yeah, I know that," Ruff said, but is it *big* enough? By that I mean, will it just sink when we drive the Tuckers' wagon onto it? I'll bet that wagon is heavier than anything that raft has ever carried across the river."

"I hadn't even thought of that," Dixie admitted. "Do you really think it could sink?"

"It's possible," Ruff said. "Either that, or the logs could separate because of the weight. In either case, it would be a disaster."

"We can't let them risk the lives of those children," Dixie said. "So maybe we should take them, Miss Tucker, and our horses across in one load and the wagon all by itself."

"Sounds good to me," Ruff said.

They waited until the Tucker wagon came rolling up and presented their concerns to the reverend. Tucker waved them aside.

"There's nothing to worry about," he said. "These ferries routinely carry heavy loads across rivers."

"Even so," Ruff said, "we still have to take two loads across. I'd say it'd be safer for the women and children to go over with the horses."

"The Lord isn't going to let us get drowned in the Red River," Tucker said, sounding a little annoyed.

Fortunately, Anna could see the logic of having her children go with a lighter and less risky load. "Mr. Ballou is right," she said. "The children will be safer crossing without our wagon."

"There's still another problem," Ruff said, "and that's the matter of payment. I'm sure that the price won't be cheap, and I assume we're all dead broke."

"Hmmm," Tucker said. "Perhaps the man is a Christian and will donate his services."

"Maybe," Dixie said, sounding as doubtful as Ruff felt.
Their doubts proved well founded because, when they

arrived at the ferryman's little shack, they found him to be drinking whiskey from a jar and possessing a most un-Christian attitude.

"No money, no payment," the tall, dirty ferryman said, spitting a stream of tobacco at Ruff's feet.

"How much is the charge?"

The ferryman studied them, his eyes calculating the amount of money he could extract. "Two dollars for that big old . . . what the hell is that thing?"

"It's a wagon," Reverend Moody Tucker snapped. "Anyone can see that!"

"Don't look like any wagon I ever saw before."

"I expanded it somewhat," the reverend said, "to meet the needs of my large family."

The man had been sitting on a chair leaning against his shack. All of a sudden, he pushed to his feet and without a word, shuffled around the Tucker wagon.

He kept shaking his head in disapproval and when he returned to them, he looked at the reverend, spat a stream of tobacco between his feet, and said, "That son of a bitch is a monstrosity and I don't believe I'd want to bother with it for no amount of goddamn money."

Ruff blinked and the reverend paled slightly. His huge fists shot out and he grabbed the ferryman by his ears and lifted him completely off the ground. Like a puppy who'd peed on the bed or a nice rug or something. The man screeched and clawed for a knife stuck in his belt but the reverend shook him and threw him up against the shack so hard he crashed through the wall.

Ruff and Dixie were too stunned to react but Anna wasn't. "Mr. Tucker!" she cried. "Now that was *not* the Christian thing to do! Go into that . . . that place and apolgize to that man right this minute."

"I will not!" Tucker's eyes blazed and did not look

Christian at all. In fact, Ruff thought he saw something quite the opposite.

The reverend ducked through the wall, knocking more boards aside. From the dim recesses of the shack, they heard a screech of pain, then a hissing sound, and finally the ferryman cried, "All right! For the love of God, have mercy! I'll do it fer nothin'!"

"Your reward will most certainly be in heaven," Tucker said, his voice turning smooth and sympathetic. "Now, can we get started, please?"

"Getting started" was not all that easy. Ruff had a dutch of a time making High Fire step onto the huge raft. When the thing bobbed slightly, Ruff thought his high-strung young Thoroughbred stallion was going to throw himself overboard. It took every bit of Ruff's ability and soothing horse talk to calm the stallion. Old High Man must have boarded a boat or raft sometime in his life because he was much calmer, and the sensible mares simply walked onto the raft as if they'd been doing it every day of their lives.

"All right," Ruff said, "Let's get Mrs. Tucker and the children aboard."

"How are we going to do this?" Tucker asked.

"You stay here and I'll go across now," Ruff said, "then come back and help you with the wagon."

"That won't be necessary," Tucker said quickly. "If indeed our wagon is dangerously overweight for this crossing, then I prefer to make the crossing alone."

"But you can't swim!" Anna cried. "Moody, if anything goes wrong, you'd sink like a stone."

"You'd better come back and return again with him," Dixie suggested.

Ruff nodded in agreement. When all was ready, two big Kentucky mules were hitched up to the cable and pulleys.

Despite the ferryman's dull appearance, the system he'd devised looked as if it would work quite well with the help of the big mules.

"Let's go," Ruff said, removing his hat and waving it when everyone and everything was set.

"Hee-yah!" the ferryman shouted, leading the mules away from the bank as the raft began to be pulled across the river.

Ruff and Dixie held their horses while the raft made its slow crossing. The river was about a hundred yards across, sluggish and dull red with suspended clay. It appeared slow and languid but Ruff suspected from the way its surface rippled that its bottom was treacherous with sunken logs and it had a powerful undercurrent.

"Hang on, children," he said as the raft bumped over something unseen, and continued across the river until the raft finally touched the opposite bank.

To disembark, they simply untied a section of border chain and led their horses onto the soil of Texas. Ruff stomped the earth. "Texas! "I always wanted to set foot on it!"

"Looks just like Oklahoma to me," Dixie said, leading the mares off the raft.

Ruff took a deep breath, then led the two stallions over to a grove of cottonwood trees and tied them far enough apart so that they wouldn't quarrel while he returned to the other side of the river to rejoin Reverend Tucker and his monstrous wagon.

Just before he stepped back onto the raft, Mrs. Tucker finished depositing her children on the bank and hurried over to say, "I hope that Mr. Tucker's terrible behavior didn't shock you too much. He has an awful temper, it's the biggest cross he bears."

The woman looked quite upset, so Ruff said, "To be

honest with you, ma'am, I sort of appreciate knowing that
he has a few of the more common human failings."

"Oh," Anna Tucker said quickly, "he does! You know,
before he became a man of the cloth, he had a very worldly
background."

"Really?" Ruff said, feeling the raft leave the bank and
start to glide back across the Red River.

"Oh yes, but don't tell him that I told you so!"

"No, ma'am!" Ruff called back. It actually tickled Ruff's
fancy to think of the reverend as a man possessing normal
human failings. Ruff had never put much thought to the
background of religious personages, realizing he'd assumed
they had all been little saints before dedicating their lives to
the service of God and their fellow man. Now he saw the
matter in a far different light. Reverend Moody Tucker had
his own human weaknesses just like everyone else.

Ruff was still marveling at this simple but profound
discovery when the raft touched back upon the Oklahoma
side of the river.

"Stand aside!" Tucker yelled, driving his wagon down
the bank and onto the raft.

Ruff jumped aside. The two draft horses didn't like the
feel of the raft at all, and when the front wheels of the
wagon pressed mightily upon the raft, it actually tilted.

The draft horses tried to whirl and jump into the river, but
Ruff managed to get them calmed. He realized that his pulse
was racing as he led the horses forward until the front end
of the raft settled back to the water. However, the Tucker
wagon was so heavy that the raft sank almost to the level
of the river's surface. Water flowed across the logs and the
horses rolled their eyes in fear.

"Get it off!" the ferryman cried. "It's too damned heavy!"

Ruff was of the same opinion and yet, it was clear that
it would be impossible to back the team and the wagon off

the raft and up the steep bank. And even if they could, what then? They'd still have to figure out some way to cross the Red River.

"We're going to have to try and go on across," Ruff shouted up to the ferryman. "Take it slow!"

The ferryman cursed but Ruff didn't hear the man. He was too busy trying to calm the draft horses, who were highly agitated by the water and unstable footing. Ruff talked to the horses in a mixture of English and Cherokee words much like what his father had always used. The words by themselves didn't make any sense, but they rarely failed to calm livestock.

"What can I do to help!" Reverend Tucker shouted down to him from his makeshift wagon seat.

"Nothing, just stay put and be ready to drive this wagon up the far bank the moment it touches Texas soil."

Ruff heard the ferryman yell at his big mules and saw their muscles bunch with exertion. The cable went taut and the raft eased into the current. Ruff wiped a sheen of nervous sweat from his brow and stayed close to the two draft horses. He found himself saying a little prayer as their raft struggled deeper into the river, tasting its mettle and being pushed so hard by the current that the steel cable yawed badly downriver.

Ruff couldn't tear his eyes off the cable. He could actually hear the thing whine as they neared the center of the river and the tension became nearly unbearable. And then, Ruff's worst fears came to pass. He heard a shout from the ferryman and saw the Texas stanchion to which the cable was attached suddenly give way under the tremendous exertion it was bearing. The stanchion leaned downriver like a falling drunk and then jerked completely out of the Texas riverbank, spinning end over end halfway across the Red River.

The effect was instant and disastrous. The raft whipped downriver. Even to that point, they were still erect but when the raft struck the end of the cable still anchored in Oklahoma, the raft went airborne—wagon, horses, and all. Ruff glanced up to see the huge double-decked wagon coming down like a falling mountain. When he struck the water, he swam for the river's bottom, going deep and remaining underwater as long as possible, unable to even imagine what was happening on the surface. When he could no longer hold his breath, Ruff clawed to the surface. He saw the horses drowning in their harness.

"Reverend!" he shouted.

Tucker rose slightly. He was clinging to one of the horses, his eyes round with shock as he stared at his over-turned wagon as it came barreling down the river at them, rolling and ripping to pieces.

Ruff swam with all his might. When he reached the thrashing, terror-filled horses, he used his knife to quickly cut them free. "Hang on!" he yelled at the reverend.

He needn't have worried. Now that the draft horses were free, they struck out powerfully, and both Ruff and Tucker clung to their tails. For a few terrible moments, Ruff didn't think that they were going to be able to avoid being driven under by the wagon. But somehow they just managed to get out of its path. The wagon was spinning apart along the surface and spewing Tucker junk as it careened on down the Red River while Ruff and Tucker let the draft horses pull them into the shore.

Dixie, Anna Tucker and a passel of crying children dragged them out of the water.

"Dear Lord, I thought we'd lost you both!" Anna cried, hugging the reverend.

Ruff heard wood rip. He pushed to his elbows and watched as the ugliest wagon he'd ever laid eyes upon sailed around a bend in the river to disappear on its way to the Gulf of Mexico.

"It guess it just wasn't our time," he said with a shake of his head.

Reverend Tucker crawled over to him. The man's face was very pale and he was shaking either from the cold or the effects of the ordeal they'd just survived.

"God almighty and you saved this sinner's life," he breathed, crushing Ruff in a bear hug. "If you hadn't cut the horses loose, we'd have been dragged under."

Ruff slapped the man's broad back and said, "You'd have done the same thing for me—if you could only swim a lick."

For some reason, the reverend thought this tremendously funny. He began to laugh. Anna began to laugh and then the Tucker children laughed. Finally, Ruff and Dixie began to laugh, too, though Ruff thought they must have all been gripped by a touch of madness.

SIX

The two draft horses and the Ballou mares carried the Tucker family south from the Red River into the rolling grass and forestlands of northeastern Texas.

"The Lord always has his own reasons," Tucker would say each night when they made camp. "He had a reason for us losing everything in the Red River, including most of the dogs and goats."

Ruff would nod his head, unwilling to argue about Divine Providence. However, he could not imagine what kind of a "reason" any loving God could have for sweeping away what few belongings the Tucker family had owned. If it had not been for the food and goods that he and Dixie carried, as well as for a couple of surviving goats they could slaughter, their losses would have been devastating. As it was, Ruff spent the last two hours of daylight hunting antelope, rabbit, prairie chickens, snakes, and any other thing that would provide meat to supplement their sparse fare.

One evening just at sundown Ruff and Tucker flushed two rabbits who bolted from cover and began to zigzag across the prairie. Ruff's hand flashed to the six-gun on his hip, and the Colt in his fist bucked twice in rapid succession. The rabbits both went into a rolling, kicking dive.

The reverend whistled and said, "You are quite an expert with that six-gun, aren't you."

"I usually hit what I aim for."

"I can see that. A man who can draw and shoot like that must have practiced a great deal."

"Some."

"That kind of shooting, Brother, will get you into trouble."

"Wrong," Ruff said, "it will put rabbit meat in our bellies."

The reverend allowed himself a smile. "That, too. However, I think that you did not learn to use a gun like that for the purpose of shooting rabbits."

Ruff looked deep into Moody Tucker's eyes. "If you're asking me if I've killed men, I have. But never in anger and always in self-defense."

The reverend studied him for a minute and then said, "I believe that. And I never considered otherwise. It just—"

"What?"

"It saddens me because we both know you learned to handle a gun in such a manner in order to shoot men— not rabbits."

Ruff couldn't honestly argue the point. "Reverend, my father died by the gun. He was shot down by a Confederate officer because he was old and slow and insisted on carrying a pepperbox pistol instead of a Colt. Maybe if I'd been a little quicker on the draw, my father would still be alive."

"You killed his murderer anyway, didn't you?"

"Yeah," Ruff said, "but it gave me no pleasure. In fact, it put a curse on our family name. Some of that Confederate captain's men escaped the gunfight and, of course, they had no choice but to claim that the Ballou family ambushed them. So we became traitors to the Confederacy even though I lost three brothers wearing gray officer's uniforms."

"I see. And is there nothing that you can do to clear your family name?"

"No," Ruff said. "All the other parties are dead or scattered. For all I know, we are still being hunted."

"Then I'm glad we are on our merry way to Texas." The reverend gazed to the south. "I like the look and feel of this country. Do you?"

"Very much."

"Good! Let's pray that this land will bring us all peace."

Ruff couldn't help himself, he had to chuckle. "Reverend, Texas has never been 'peaceful.' It's as blood bought as any land in the West. I don't guess I need to tell you about all the killing done by Mexicans, Americans, and Indians."

"No." The reverend's smile dissolved. "I don't believe you do."

Ruff and Tucker locked eyes for a long minute and then Ruff said, "We still have about a half hour before sundown to hunt enough rabbit for everyone. We'd better collect the pair I just shot, though."

Ruff started to dismount but Tucker jumped off his draft horse and went to retrieve the dead rabbits. Picking both up by the hind legs, he walked back to the horses. "Be a nice change from goat meat."

"Those two rabbits won't feed us all," Ruff said, watching the sun die in the western horizon. "Let's keep riding until it gets too dark to see."

The reverend nodded and handed the rabbits over to Ruff. He grinned sheepishly, then went to mount his big draft horse. Tucker stood a little over six feet but the backbone of his draft horse was still chest high. The heavyset man searched in vain for a rock to help him get a leg up, but seeing nothing to step onto, he sighed. "Here goes."

Ruff bit back a grin. He'd seen the reverend in this situation before and the results were amusing and predictable.

"Hmmph!" the reverend grunted, throwing himself off

the ground, grabbing at the horse's withers and trying to elevate his bulk. The horse staggered, braced its legs apart, and waited as the reverend dropped back to the ground. Tucker attempted to mount three more times and then, gasping and red faced, he looked up at Ruff, a plea in his pale blue eyes.

"It says that pride goeth before a fall, Brother Ballou, but I can't even jump high enough to fall!"

Ruff chuckled and so did Tucker. During this first week of travel, the two of them had settled into a comfortable relationship based on mutual respect. Ruff dismounted and walked over to the exasperated draft horse.

"It's the size of this horse that's the problem," he said graciously. "I couldn't begin to jump that high, either. Maybe you ought to tie a stepping-stone around this big fellow's neck."

Tucker snorted with derision. "A stepping-stone? Ha! And I've seen you vault onto that bareback Thoroughbred like a Comanche Indian."

"Your horse is taller."

"Only a shade."

"Sometimes that's all the difference." Ruff cupped his hands and the reverend placed his left foot into them and Ruff heaved him up. Unfortunately, he used too much muscle and Tucker flipped completely over the horse and crashed down on the other side.

"Ugggh!" the man gasped, and then began to suck desperately for air.

Ruff hurried around to the other side. The draft horse didn't move. In fact, its eyelids were drooping because it was worn out after a long day of travel. The reverend was pale and shaken.

"Are you all right!" Ruff asked.

"Help me up," the reverend wheezed.

Ruff assisted the man to his feet. Tucker was bent over, fighting to refill his lungs.

"Maybe we'd better walk the horses on back to camp."

But the reverend shook his head. "Let's see if we can bag a few more rabbits or something. The wife and the children are losing weight before my very eyes."

Ruff didn't say that it was probably just as well. The reverend and his wife had visibly slimmed down in the week since they'd lost everything in the Red River. This family was in no danger of starving.

"Are you sure?"

"Yes."

"All right," Ruff said. "Give me your foot."

"Not so damned hard this time, okay?"

Ruff grinned. "Okay."

He managed to get the reverend back on his horse and then Ruff remounted High Fire. They rode straight into the dying sun and an ocean of liquid gold. The air was still and birds flitted through the grass seeking a nest for the night.

Ruff liked everything he saw about this country. It was big shouldered, green and fertile. It was still mostly open land because the Comanche yet remained the lords of these plains due to the small groupings of white people in small settlements hugging the rivers, choosing to be near the protection of a few Army outposts.

But the days of the Plains Indian and the vast herds of buffalo were almost history. Their buffalo herds had been largely wiped out this far south and the Indians who had depended upon them for their food, shelter, and way of life were now often hungry and desperate. They stole cattle and horses. They traded their bounty for a few final years of freedom and survival.

Ruff saw buffalo bones and buffalo wallows everywhere. And at night when he closed his eyes, he could still *smell* the buffalo—as if they had become a part of the earth and were lying just below its rich, dark soil, waiting to spring to life reborn and flood across the plains, like muddy water bursting over the Tennessee River banks in springtime.

Ruff saw a huge rattlesnake moving through the grass about twenty yards off. It had heard the vibrations of their approaching horses and was trying to escape. Ruff drew his gun. "Snake meat is a favorite of mine."

To his surprise, the reverend said, "The serpent is accursed by the Lord, may I?"

"What?"

"Use your gun to dispatch the vile creature?"

Ruff shrugged his shoulders. He just hoped that the reverend did not waste all six bullets and scare off any other game they might have a chance of bagging this evening.

Tucker accepted the pistol. He reined his horse in, aimed, and fired. To Ruff's amazement, the head of the snake disappeared, leaving a bloody, wiggling stump.

"Holy Moses!" Ruff exclaimed. "That was some shooting! Where'd you ever learn to use a pistol like that?"

The reverend sighed. "I was not always a Christian. In fact, I was a Mississippi riverboat gambler during my twenties and early thirties. It's a profession that requires some degree of skill with a weapon."

"But a while back, you were critical of my ability."

"Not critical," the reverend said, "just concerned. Besides, I never learned the fast draw. Most of the scrapes I was in were at close range. I am more familiar with a derringer than a Colt. And like your father, I also had a penchant for the pepperbox. There was just something about six barrels staring at a man that had a distinct calming and reasoning effect."

"Well, I'll be!" Ruff said, tickled beyond measure. "So you were a gambler!"

"I *am* a gambler," Tucker said. "It and my temper are two crosses I will always have to bear—as my wife will readily tell you."

Ruff dismounted and walked over to the wriggling snake. He hoisted it aloft, and it was a yard long. "Five pounds if he's an ounce. You or any of your family ever eat snake meat?"

"No."

"Tastes a little like chicken," Ruff said, carrying the dead serpent over to his horse. High Fire snorted with fear and rolled his eyes but Ruff managed to get back into the saddle.

"You shot him, you carry him, Reverend."

Tucker nodded and traded Ruff back his gun for the snake. "He is a big devil, isn't he. Bony?"

"No," Ruff said. "We'll skin him and roast him on willow sticks laid across rocks over our campfire. Along with the rabbits, we'll eat well tonight."

"Amen," the reverend said, "the Lord does provide."

That night, Ruff and Dixie had some fun teasing the Tucker family about the healthful benefits of eating rattlesnake meat. "Eat enough of it," Ruff said to the children with a wink to the grown-ups, "and you'll grow rattles on your little behinds."

"Rufus!" Dixie protested when the children gaped. "Don't you dare tell them such awful stories."

But Ruff wasn't listening. In particular he was speaking to six-year-old Monica, among his favorites. "And even if you eat just a little snake meat, tomorrow you'll be able to slither through the grass as easy as anything."

"Ruff!"

He laughed. "All right. No more."

Anna Tucker seemed relieved to hear this. "You have quite an imagination with children, Ruff. Quite an imagination. Someday, you'll make a very . . . interesting father."

Ruff's smile faded as the image of Thia rushed upon him unbidden. His children should also have been *her* children.

Ruff looked up at Anna and said, "Maybe I won't ever have any children. But I sure do enjoy yours."

She smiled. "And we are enjoying this snake meat. In fact, I like it even better than the rabbit."

"Me too," Monica said, her sentiments echoed by most of her brothers and sisters.

"Ruff, how far do you think we've come?" Tucker asked.

"I'd say we're almost a hundred miles south of the Red River. From what I've been told, we must be nearing the the Trinity River."

"Is it as big as the Red?" Tucker asked, his face tensing with concern.

"No," Ruff said. "I don't think so. And neither is the Brazos. We'll also have to cross it before we reach Austin."

"Thank heavens for small rivers," Anna Tucker said.

Ruff nodded. He saw no point in telling anyone that the same man who had told him about the rivers had also warned that the Comanche were riding and raiding in this part of the country, even more so to the south. And once or twice, Ruff had ridden off a ways to discover the ashes and charred bones of what he was certain were Indian campfires.

They came upon the Trinity River the very next afternoon and without a huge double-decked wagon, a printing press, and about a ton of furniture and personal belongings to ferry, they swam the river with ease.

Once on the other side, they saw a few men and a pair of high-sided wagons camped nearby. The men waved and shouted, gesturing for them to come and join them, but Ruff voiced his reservations.

"I'll go see what I can find out," he said, "but I think we ought to steer clear of that bunch."

"But why?" Dixie asked.

"Look at them," Ruff said. "Unless I miss my bet, they're bone pickers."

"Bone pickers?"

"That's right. I've heard of them. Most often, they used to be buffalo hunters and hiders. Now that they've wiped out almost all of the buffalo herds in this part of the country, they've taken to collecting their bones."

Reverend Tucker scratched his chin. "Maybe you and I *both* ought to talk to them."

"Better if I went alone," Ruff said, "and you stayed with the women and children."

"Why don't we just go on and ignore them?" Dixie suggested.

"We could try it," Ruff said, "but I think they'd take offense and come after us. And even if they did not, we need to learn something about the Comanche situation between here and Austin."

Ruff dismounted and checked his cinch. He reached into his saddlebag and drew out a second Army Colt. He checked the loads and primer caps, then shoved the weapon in his waistband.

"It'll be fine," he said to Dixie. "These men are probably interested in knowing whether or not we've seen Comanche between here and the Red River."

"You got an extra pistol in that saddlebag?" Tucker asked quietly as he came over to stand beside Ruff.

"Yes," Ruff said, "a couple."

Tucker took both. "I'm not going to ask you where you got these," he said. "But if there's any indication that you might be riding into trouble, you wheel that Thoroughbred horse around and you come tearing back here just as fast as you can. We can take cover here in the trees and defend ourselves."

"I'll do it," Ruff promised, mounting his stallion. He tipped his hat to them and touched his heels to the flanks of his horse. High Fire burst into a gallop and carried him swiftly down the riverbank until he came to the edge of the camp.

"Got any whiskey?" a thin, turkey-necked man asked hopefully as three others even more filthy than he was came forward to stare at Ruff and his fine stallion.

"No whiskey," Ruff said, wanting to sound poor, "and no food or money. We lost everything trying to cross the Red River a week or so back."

"Where'd you cross?"

"At the ferry."

"Well, then . . ."

"The cable broke and the raft flipped."

At this news, the four men began to giggle and then guffaw as if that were the most hilarious thing they'd ever heard. Ruff felt his hackles rising but he stayed on his horse and kept a straight face.

When the laughter finally died, he said, "We're heading for Austin. I suppose that dirt track leading south-southwest is the road?"

"Yep. Road forks about three days south of here, one going down to Houston, the other to Austin. Stay to the right and hope you don't run into any Comanche that are layin' for the kind of poor outfit you be leadin'."

"You seen Comanche?"

The man who appeared to be the leader was in his forties, with a battered hat, a salt-and-pepper beard, and wearing blood-and grease-stained clothes. He had deep-set eyes, a gun on his hip, and a way of looking at a man that made him squirm.

"We see Comanche off and on wherever we roam out in this part of Texas. That's why we got buffalo rifles and Spencer repeating rifles. You got a nice-lookin' one, from what I can see."

Ruff did not look down at the rifle attached to his saddle. He had the feeling that it would be a mistake to look anywhere but directly at the man who had now stepped forward staring at High Fire with real interest.

"It's broken," Ruff said, "the Spencer is broken."

"Maybe we could fix it for you."

"Nope." Ruff wanted to change the subject. "I can smell those buffalo bones you're collecting. What do people buy them for?"

"Back east they grind 'em to powder, then use it to make the rich ladies bone china," the man said. "And for fertilizer. That's a hoot, ain't it? Out west, a man can find himself up to his neck in cow, horse, or buffalo dump, back east they *pay* for the damned stuff."

"Looks like a hard, dangerous way to make a living."

"All ways are hard and dangerous in Texas," the man said. He squinted. "Why don't you show me that busted Spencer rifle?"

Ruff saw the other three men tense and noted how their dirty paws inched closer to their guns.

The black eyes of the leader squeezed into slits and he actually smiled. "I think you'd best hand it over, stranger. And I sure do like the looks of that stud horse you're ridin'. Why don't you stand down."

Ruff's heart began to bang against the insides of his ribs. He shifted in his saddle and then he expelled a deep breath. "All right."

Only instead of reaching for the Spencer, his hand flashed toward his gun butt and he dragged the Colt up in the wink of an eye. It locked on the bearded man's chest and the sound of the hammer cocking seemed louder than a hammer striking an anvil.

The four men started to claw for their guns but then the bearded man that Ruff was about to shoot cried, "No!"

Ruff held his gun steady although he was quaking inside. "I'm backing my horse out of here," he said. "But first, spread-eagle facedown on the ground."

"In hell we will!" the leader choked.

"That's up to you," Ruff said. "You'll be dead and so will at least two more of you before I'm finished. So either get down or make your play."

"He's just a kid!" one of the men hissed. "Still green behind the ears! We can take him!"

But after staring into Ruff's eyes for a moment, the leader shook his head. "He's green, but I think any man who can shuck a pistol that fast also knows how to use it. Let's do as he says."

"But . . ."

"Do it, dammit! I'm the first one he'll shoot!"

The four bone pickers dropped to the ground, cursing.

"Spread-eagle!" Ruff commanded.

"You son of a bitch," the leader hissed, "you're in *Texas* now! And you ain't seen the last of us!"

Ruff guessed that was probably true. He also knew that the only intelligent thing to do now would be to shoot all four. But he couldn't do that, for his own fool code of honor didn't allow for executions.

"Like I said," Ruff told them as he backed his stallion away with his gun still on the four, "we lost everything of value in the Red River."

"You got horses, women, and weapons, you lanky son of a bitch!"

"And a bullet waiting if you try and take them," Ruff yelled as he reined High Fire around and went racing away.

Before he had gone a quarter mile the bone pickers had fired their buffalo rifles. The first bullet whistled past Ruff's face so close that he knew that he or High Fire would be killed in the next few moments unless he rode like a crazy man. So he reined to the left and a few moments later, to the right as three more heavy lead balls sought to kill him or his stallion.

When Ruff arrived back at camp, Tucker had the women, children and horses already hidden in the cottonwood trees. The reverend shouted, "I take it they weren't Christians!"

Ruff pulled High Fire into the woods. He jumped out of his saddle and grabbed his Spencer. "They're just a bunch of thieves and murderers," he said. "Same as the trash and deserters we knew in the South."

"What happens now?"

"Your guess is as good as mine. Reverend, are you going to start praying again?"

"Yes."

"But you'll fight if prayer doesn't work, won't you?"

Tucker nodded his double chins. "I'll fight," he vowed, a Colt clenched in either fist. "And, Brother Ballou—know this—if I can't save their souls, I'll send 'em straight to hell!"

Ruff liked that a lot. And despite his earliest reservations, the Reverend Moody Tucker was a man proving himself worth knowing and calling friend.

SEVEN

They didn't have long to wait to find out what the
bone pickers would do next. The four filthy men hitched
their two high-sided wagons up to eight mules and drove
them forward, side by side, four mules to each wagon,
two men on each driver's seat, big buffalo rifles at the
ready.

"We're in for it now," Dixie warned, drawing her six-
gun.

The Reverend Tucker knelt and bowed his head and so
did his family. "Lord, we don't want a fight. We're peaceful
people and all life is precious—ours included! So I'll fight
and if you'll protect the missus and the children, it won't
matter if I get shot. And—"

"Reverend!" Ruff called, "they're almost into their buffalo rifle range. Get your family and those draft horses farther
back in trees right now!"

"Amen!"

The bone pickers kept coming and when they were still
just out of the Spencer's range, they pulled in their wagons
and raised their big rifles—and waited, still as statues.

"What are they doing?" Dixie asked.

"They're expert marksmen waiting for one of us to show
ourselves," Ruff replied. "But stay covered and we'll make

71

them keep waiting until they lose their patience and come into *our* rifle range."

An hour passed and the bone pickers finally began to jaw at each other. They were a good four hundred yards distant and Ruff could hear them arguing, though he could not distinguish their words.

"Here they come again," Reverend Tucker said, clutching two six-guns.

"They'll just keep coming and . . ."

Whatever Ruff was about to say next was forgotten when he saw all four men leap onto their cargo of bones so that only the tops of their heads and their big rifles were showing.

"They've done this before," Ruff said in a tight voice. "They'll keep driving forward until we show ourselves, and then they'll try to pick us off."

"So what do we do!" Dixie exclaimed.

"We let them come right up to the edge of this stand of cottonwoods," Ruff said, motioning them to retreat with him farther into the trees. "They can't bring the wagons in here and that means they'll have to jump out of their wagons. That's when we'll take them."

Ruff waited until he figured out about where the wagons would have to stop. "We need to spread out and catch them in a cross fire. When they come around the sides, that's when we catch them in our cross fire."

Dixie and the reverend nodded. Both looked plenty worried but determined. Ruff knew that they'd do fine. "I've got a repeating rifle so I'll go off by myself. Dixie, you and the reverend circle in the opposite direction."

Ruff sprinted through the trees until he found what he hoped was a good vantage point. Out on the grasslands, the two wagons kept rolling forward, their passengers frantically searching for a target. Suddenly, the mules reached the

edge of the trees and could go no farther. Ruff saw bones
spill out the rear of both wagons and then the four men
jumped down and started to move.

Ruff took aim and his first bullet found its mark as a
man crashed back against his wagon. The bone pickers
froze in panic just as Dixie and Tucker opened fire from
another vantage point. The men realized they were caught
in a deadly cross fire. Ruff would have expected them to
leap back into the cover of their wagons, but instead they
bolted for the trees.

Another man was hit in the shoulder. He spun completely
around, and that saved his life because Ruff's bullet would
have drilled him through the chest. Then, in a hail of bullets,
the wounded man staggered into the cottonwood grove.
Ruff shot another man who thought that he was covered
by a slender tree.

Ruff dropped his rifle and plunged forward, intent on
finishing off the two survivors before they could reach
Tucker and Dixie, or worse yet, find Mrs. Tucker and
the children. He slammed through the barrier of brush
and fought his way through thickets, hearing the staccato
of gunfire.

"Dixie!" he shouted, vaulting a rotting log to nearly land
on the bone picker with the bullet in his shoulder.

Ruff snapped his pistol up and fired. He missed and dived
for cover, rolling and firing at the same time. This second
bullet found its mark and the wounded man slumped and
was still. Ruff climbed to his feet hearing a succession of
rapid gunshots. He threw himself forward, expecting to find
Dixie or the reverend both dead. Instead, he found the
bearded leader thrashing about on a carpet of decaying
leaves.

"The Lord have mercy on your soul, Brother!" Reverend
Tucker cried, kneeling beside the dying man. "Do you

repent before God and his witness? Do you ask forgiveness for the eternal salvation of your soul?"

"Guhhh . . ."

The reverend leaned closer. "Yes, Brother! Ask His forgiveness and it will be received and you shall dwell in the house of the Lord always!"

"Guhh . . . oh to hell!" the bearded man choked. He even attempted to spit on the reverend but only managed to drool before he died with a convulsive shudder.

The reverend bowed his head and prayed in silence. Ruff walked over to Dixie and helped her to her feet. "You all right?"

"Yes," she whispered. "I shot one, he shot this man. I didn't see him and he'd have put a bullet in my back if it hadn't been for Reverend Tucker."

Ruff draped his arm around his sister's shoulder and led her away. He'd be damned if he would pray over the body of a man who'd almost shot Dixie in the back.

That night they slept badly and in the morning, they buried the four bone pickers in the soft, damp soil beside the gentle Trinity River. The Tucker children were very somber and the smaller ones were actually tearful. The reverend spoke for nearly an hour on the wages of sin and the sanctity of life. Ruff could see that the killing of men had shaken him badly, even though it might not have during his years as a riverboat gambler on the Mississippi.

When the service was over, the reverend insisted that the graves be marked with crosses. Ruff was annoyed. "These men were murderers who deserve nothing."

"Either you can make the crosses or I will," Tucker replied.

"I'll do it," Ruff growled. He found some strips of rawhide and crawled up into a bone wagon and located suitable specimens. Long leg bones made the upper stand, and the cross pieces were shorter bones. Ruff finished the four highly unusual crosses and jammed each into the soft earth over the graves. The entire job took him less than half an hour.

"Satisfied?" he asked the reverend.

"Not very."

"We should move on," Ruff said. "And we need to take the bone wagons."

Tucker stared at him. "And why in the world would we do that!"

"The wagons are valuable and so is the cargo. We can probably sell both in Austin or some other settlement for a couple hundred dollars, assuming both teams of mules are sound."

The reverend was appalled. "We will have no part of that! Horses, wagons, rifles—any of it!"

Ruff's temper flared. "Don't be a fool! You need those things! They're worth more than what you lost in the Red River. When you get to Austin, you'll have a stake!"

"The Lord *will* provide!"

"That's right, he will," Ruff argued hotly, "but he also helps those who help themselves."

The reverend blinked. "So," he said, lowering his voice, "you acutally have had some Bible teaching."

Ruff relaxed. "A little. Not much, but enough to know that it is no sin to take what he gives, as well as accept what he takes. You've got to be willing to do both, Reverend Tucker. If not for yourself, then for your family."

"I'm not sure I agree."

"If you don't," Dixie said, jumping into the conversation, "then it'd be your pride stopping you, Reverend. And you know it says that pride cometh before a fall."

The reverend shook his head and looked over at his wife

and children. "I don't know," he said, "I'm beginning to wonder if the Lord is testing me."

"Maybe he is," Ruff said, "and maybe he's giving us a way to protect ourselves if we are attacked by Comanche before we reach Austin."

The reverend blinked. "What does that mean?"

"It means that those foul bone wagons are like little fortresses. You saw how those four men used them."

"Yes, but . . ."

"I expect that they've used them before that way against attack from Indians. They could stay inside and fire all those rifles they owned and it would be almost impossible to dislodge them."

Ruff looked at Dixie. "Those bone wagons might look and smell bad, but they could also save our scalps."

"I agree."

They both stared at Reverend Tucker, who in turn looked at his wife and children. "All right," he finally relented, "we'll take the wagons and their belongings, but when we reach Austin, we'll sell everything and donate the proceeds to some worthy charity!"

"Charity," Ruff reminded the man, "begins at home."

Tucker opened his mouth to say something but his wife pressed her forefinger to her lips and Tucker clamped his mouth shut, turned, and stomped away.

"He's not only got a temper," Ruff said to the woman, "but he's got a stubborn streak a mile wide."

"So you've noticed," she said before going to console her troubled husband.

The rest of the day was somber and that evening, when they made camp some fifteen miles south of the Trinity River, there was little conversation and everyone, even the children, were subdued.

But in the morning, while he hitched up the mules,

Ruff sensed a change of mood when the Reverend Tucker boomed, "Good morning, Rufus!"

"Morning," Ruff replied. "We've got ourselves some mighty fine mules here. They've been a little neglected but we'll do something about that."

"I'm sure you will," the reverend said. "And I want to apologize for being angry yesterday. My anger, as you probably guessed, was misdirected toward you."

"Forget it," Ruff said, finishing with one team of mules and going to the other team. "All I'm hoping for is a safe, uneventful journey the rest of the way down to Austin."

"Did those bone pickers say anything about Indians before they became aggressive?"

"Yes," Ruff admitted, "they did. I don't know how much I can take their word as truth, but they let me know that we'd probably run into Comanche before we reached safety."

Tucker bent to help Ruff with the harness. "I'd rather you not pass that troubling information on to Mrs. Tucker and the children."

"Of course not."

"Good. And I also want to thank you for pointing out to me that these wagons could be our salvation in case of an Indian attack. I'd never forgive myself if I had let my pride expose my family or yours to unnecessary danger."

"Reverend," Ruff said, finishing with the harness. "Let's just hitch those mules to these bone wagons and get them rolling south. The best thing that we can do now is to cover as much ground as possible each day and try to reach Austin as soon as we can. And don't forget that we still have to ford the Brazos River."

"Maybe we'll find another ferry."

"Maybe," Ruff said, doubting it.

A quarter hour later, they were rolling. Dixie refused to

sit on a pile of stinking bones so she rode High Man while Ruff drove the front wagon and the reverend followed along on the second wagon and his family. The bones were mostly bleached and dried so the children did not mind piling on to them. In fact, as Ruff drove along, he could hear them playing on their rolling bone pile.

They made fine time for the next several days until one afternoon, when Ruff saw a swarm of buzzards circling a few miles just up ahead.

Dixie galloped up to his side. "What do you think?"

"I don't know," Ruff said, a furrow creasing his brow. "But they're circling right over where we're heading, and I guess we'll be finding out what they are after."

"Probably a horse or a buffalo?"

"Probably," Ruff said hopefully.

It was late afternoon when he saw an abandoned Conestoga wagon surrounded by a dead, bloated team of oxen and the bodies of a man and woman impaled by Comanche lances.

Ruff's expression turned wintery. "Dixie, ride back and tell the reverend that I'm going to veer around this tragedy and that he might want to keep the sight from his smallest children."

Dixie spun the Thoroughbred around and galloped back to relay this information. She returned a few minutes later and accompanied Ruff as they skirted the scene of death by a quarter mile. They went on for another half hour and then made camp beside a small stream down in a wide arroyo, where they would be invisible to Indians or anyone else for that matter.

"I'm going back with you," the reverend announced in a firm, uncompromising voice. "I'll need to give those poor people the last rites and help you bury them."

Ruff knew better than to argue, even though it bothered

him to leave Dixie and the Tucker brood largely unprotected. He went to Dixie and said, "If you see any hint of trouble, fire warning shots. We'll be able to get back here in just a few minutes on horseback."

"All right. But I wish I could go with you."

"I know," Ruff said, "but you can serve best by staying with Mrs. Tucker and the children."

Splashed in the shimmering rays of the dying sun, Ruff and Tucker hurried back to the death camp. Their horses snorted with fear, rolling their eyes and not wanting to move in close. The gory-beaked buzzards squawked and hissed, flapping their wings. Ruff had to grab a stick and drive them off the carcasses.

He had seen much death in the Civil War, but witnessing a man and his wife pinned to the earth with Comanche lances hit him like a powerful body blow. He kept seeing Dixie or Mrs. Tucker instead of the poor woman whose mouth gaped and whose eyes bugged with glazed terror.

Ruff made a quick inspection of the camp. Everything was ransacked. A trunk of clothes had been pulled from the wagon and its contents scattered everywhere. All dishes and glassware were shattered and the furniture smashed to bits. A large, gray-muzzled old dog lay riddled with arrows.

"Ruff!" the reverend called. "Come here, quick!"

Ruff hurried over to the man and stared at a hand-carved pistol. "They had a child!" Tucker cried, his face ashen with shock.

Ruff stared at the doll and then went back into the wagon. Sure enough, he found a box of toys and children's clothing. From the toys, he guessed that the child was about five or six years old and had been a boy.

After searching a little more, Ruff came back to the reverend and said, "They must have taken him."

"Yes," Tucker said. "Let's bury these poor souls."

Ruff found a shovel and used it to good advantage. He and the reverend worked fast, both fearing that the Indians might be nearby. Once, Tucker said, "How long ago do you think this tragedy occurred?"

"A day. No more, probably no less."

"I'm scared to death," Tucker admitted. "Not for myself, but for my family. We should never have come to Texas."

"We're going to make it," Ruff said. "Because we have to."

"But what . . . never mind."

They laid the man and the woman into the same grave and covered them fast. The reverend's eulogy was short and by the time it was over, the sun was down and darkness blanketed the land. Ruff took the shovel and a few other tools that the Indians had neither discovered nor destroyed. He had found no food, weapons, or ammunition but he did discover a stack of letters.

"We can read these when we get to Austin and they might tell us who to notify as the next of kin."

"Yes," Tucker said, using the tongue of the wagon to mount his draft horse. He kicked the animal into a gallop and Ruff raced after him.

When they rejoined the women and children, it was a reunion more typical of someone that had been gone for days instead of a few hours.

"Thank God you're safe," Ruff whispered, hugging Dixie. "No campfire tonight."

"And maybe not for the rest of the trip," Mrs. Tucker said.

"That might be best," Ruff agreed, worrying about how a constant diet of raw meat would affect the children's health. "We'll play it one day at a time."

That night, Ruff stood first guard, then Dixie took his

place at midnight, followed by the reverend until dawn. They awoke and with very few words and no hot breakfast, broke camp, emerging from hiding like frightened prairie dogs under the eye of the sun and a hawk.

EIGHT

For the next few days, they talked of little other than the poor family they'd buried and the boy who'd been kidnapped. Dixie and Mrs. Tucker were very upset and once Reverend Tucker even suggested they probably should try and rescue the poor child.

"If we left your family we'd be putting them at a terrible risk," Ruff argued. "There is nothing we can do to help the child right now."

"But if not now, then when!" the reverend exploded with exasperation. "Brother Ballou, the Christian thing to do—"

"Is to get your family to safety in Austin and then inform the Texas authorites about those killings and the child's kidnapping," Ruff interrupted. "It's the only sensible way to handle this. Besides, I have heard that the Comanche treat captive children very well."

"Ha!" Tucker cried. "Unlike our Cherokee, these Comanche are a godless people! You saw what they did to the child's parents!"

"Yes," Ruff admitted, "I did."

Ruff saw no use in pointing out to the upset minister that the Indians were being annihilated by the whites and that their main supply of food—the buffalo—was systematically being wiped off the face of the earth for the value

82

of their hides and bones. Slaughtering millions of buffalo didn't excuse murder, but it did help to explain why the Comanche, Kiowa, and other Plains Indians were so fierce in their opposition to the tide of whites that kept flooding into their traditional hunting grounds.

Two days later, they crossed a swath of churned-up grass and Ruff dismounted to study the unshod hoof marks.

"Indians?" Tucker asked.

"Yes. Indians or a band of renegades would be my guess. And they passed through here not more than a few hours ago."

Anna Tucker visibly paled. "My heavens, Rufus! What if . . ."

"We'll look for a low spot or some trees," Ruff said. "Somewhere to hole up in the daytime. Then we'll travel only at night. That will slow us down but lessen our chances of being spotted."

"What about the wheel tracks of our bone wagons?" Dixie asked. "They're visible for a mile. Even more when we roll through knee-deep grass."

"Can't be helped."

"We can leave the wagons behind," the reverend suggested.

Ruff frowned. "That's your decision, but I'd advise against it for the same reasons I talked about before. If we are attacked—"

"Never mind that," the reverend said harshly, cutting Ruff off because he did not want to scare his wife and children any more than necessary. "We'll keep the wagons."

"Good," Ruff said, stung by the man's hard tone of voice. "So let's keep moving until we find a hiding place."

They found their hiding place less than an hour later in a low valley fed by a stream choked with cottonwoods.

"We'll stay here until dark and then travel all night."

"How much farther?" Mrs. Tucker asked fretfully.

"One, maybe two nights of travel if we push it hard," Ruff replied. "But I can't say for sure."

"Thank you," she answered. "And thank you for not just abandoning my family. I know that riding those wonderful Thoroughbreds of yours, you both could have already been in Austin. I know too that you could leave us and easily outdistance any Indians we might have to face."

"We're not going to leave anyone," Ruff assured her. "And besides, without your husband, I don't think we would have survived that fight with the bone pickers along the Trinity River. So you see, we're just repaying the favor."

The woman cocked her head a little to one side. "Your name is Ruff, but you're not very rough at all inside, do you know that?"

He blushed and she noticed because she said, "See, you've just proved my words. Hard men don't blush like schoolboys. How old are you?"

"Nineteen."

Anna signed. "You've taken on a lot for such a young age. Not only with the horses, but with your sister."

"My sister is no bother," Ruff said, "in fact, lots of times, she thinks of better ways to do things. She's smart and sensible."

"Yes, but so are you."

Ruff didn't know what to say. He felt proud but all he could do was to just toe the earth around a little.

"I think," Anna said, watching her children play in the heavy woods, "that we are going to have to deal with these Comanche Indians."

"Maybe not," Ruff said. "Maybe we'll slip through."

"That's what we're praying for," Anna said, her Scandinavian blue eyes troubled, "but call it a woman's intuition or whatever you want, I am resigned to meeting those godless savages."

Ruff just nodded his head. "Well, I'd better get to taking care of the horses and the mules, Mrs. Tucker."

"And I my husband and children," she said, looking deep into his black eyes and then turning to walk away.

Dixie came over to Ruff. "I saw the expression on your face, is something wrong?"

"Nothing you don't already know about," he said. "Anna feels sure that we are going to have to fight the Comanche."

"She said that? Exactly?"

"Well, she said she was resigned to meeting those godless savages, so it was the same thing."

"Not necessarily," Dixie said.

"What does that mean?"

"It means that we might meet them but not have to fight them."

Ruff's expression clouded. "Dixie, you didn't see that dead man and his wife up close or you'd think otherwise."

Dixie said nothing before she walked off to be by herself.

It felt strange trying to sleep during the day knowing a war party of Comanche were ranging somewhere nearby. It felt strange enough that Ruff didn't get much sleep at all and he doubted that the others did, either. Certainly the children did not. Ruff could hear them singing and playing hide-and-seek in the cottonwood grove. He wished they'd be quiet but that was unrealistic. The youngest didn't understand the danger they were in, which was for the best.

Ruff kept thinking about the kidnapped child and wondering what his name was and what he looked like. Would the Comanche really treat him well? How terrified would a six-year-old white boy be of the Indians who had murdered his parents and his dog, probably before his very eyes? Ruff wished with all his heart he could do something to help the kid, but of course he could not.

It was a helpless feeling, sort of like the way he'd felt back in Tennessee when the great armies of the North were conquering the last of the Confederate armies. Or when his brother Mason had made Ruff and Houston leave to bring help, all of them knowing that there was no help available and that Mason was going to die before they could return.

Before the war, Ruff realized that he had been under some childhood illusion that he would grow up tall, strong, and invincible, like Justin Ballou. When growing up, Ruff had believed that his father could forge any situation to his iron will and that, when Ruff grew up, he could do the same. The Civil War had taught Ruff otherwise. He knew now that all men, even presidents Abraham Lincoln or Jefferson Davis, were helplessly immersed in a terrible war whose outcome and day-to-day operation were largely beyond their control.

Out here on these vast Texas plains, a small boy was kidnapped and Ruff was powerless to help him. A very large party of Comanche was nearby and Ruff could do nothing but hide in a grove of trees like a frightened rabbit in its burrow.

It was all enormously humbling. Ruff knew that he had not been able to save Thia's life and now, he was not at all sure that he could save Dixie's or anyone else's if the Comanche found them in hiding or caught them hurrying south in the dead of the night.

The day was hot, even in the shade of the trees. Now and then, Ruff would lift his hat from his eyes. He'd observe the horses and mules, then the playing children, and finally his sister, who was dozing fitfully underneath the bone wagon alongside Mrs. Tucker.

Ruff wished he could sleep because he knew that he'd need rest if he were to be alert through the long, dangerous nights ahead. But the harder he tried to sleep, the more impossible became the task. Finally, he pushed himself to his feet, grabbed his rifle, and went to the edge of the woods to survey the huge, open expanse of Texas grassland.

Big open spaces made Ruff feel uneasy. He felt much more comfortable in the eastern forests of Tennessee, where he'd been raised. In the forest, a man could hide from superior enemies. If he were stealthy and quiet, an enemy might pass within a few yards without being aware of his presence. But out here, except for the occasional stands of forest and the strips of cottonwoods to be found along the waterways, a man couldn't hide for beans. He might dip into an arroyo or low place, but he had to come out again if he wanted to make progress.

Yes, Ruff thought, he much preferred the heavy eastern woods to the open plains of the West. Perhaps that would change in time, but . . .

A scream interrupted Ruff's meditations. He whirled, half expecting to see a Comanche brave scalping one of the Tucker children. Instead, he saw the children scattering and then he heard another scream. Mrs. Tucker sat up so fast that she cracked her head on the underside of the bone wagon and opened a nasty gash in her forehead. The reverend was already coming to his feet as Ruff drew his gun and sprinted toward the sound of the screaming child.

"It's Monica!" the reverend cried, tearing through the brush like a wild man.

The child was sitting beside two of the biggest rattlesnakes Ruff had ever seen. A trickle of blood was seeping from the child's leg, another from her arm. The snakes were coiled to strike again and the child was frozen in terror.

Ruff took aim and fired his Colt just as one snake struck. His bullet kicked the viper sideways and the reverend stomped its head into the dirt with his boot. The second snake struck the reverend just above the ankle. He cried out and kicked the twisting serpent into the air. It landed in the thickets and disappeared.

Reverend Tucker scooped up his daughter and ran toward the wagon. He was limping badly. Ruff sprinted after the man. Anna Tucker, half-dazed and bleeding from a nasty gash she'd just suffered, looked wild with fear.

"What is it!"

"Rattlesnake bites," Tucker cried. "What are we going to do!"

"I . . . what's wrong with your leg!" Anna cried.

The reverend's eyes dropped to his ankle. "Anna, the serpents bit me, too."

Anna Tucker's hand fluttered to her blood-streaked face and she fainted dead away.

Ruff said, "We'll cut the wound and suck out the poison as best we can. You and the child lie down!"

The reverend nodded dumbly. He lay down, clutching Monica in his arms and at the same time trying to touch his poor wife. "What's happened to her!" he exclaimed, sitting erect to stare at the blood on his wife's face.

"She hit her head on the underside of the wagon," Dixie explained, trying to keep her own sanity as this sudden and terrible nightmare unfolded. "She's going to be all right."

The reverend nodded and lay back down, still holding Monica. The child's leg and arm were already beginning to swell badly. Ruff knew that she was at a far greater risk of dying of the snake venom than her father, who was probably five times heavier and stronger.

"We'll need to hold Monica very still," Ruff said. "Reverend, keep her steady. This will hurt."

The reverend nodded. Tears of pain and anguish for his daughter streaked his red cheeks. His lips began to move rapidly and Ruff knew the man was praying for his daughter's innocent life rather than his own.

Ruff drew his bowie knife. It seemed outlandishly large when he raised it to the girl's skinny arm. Dixie must have thought so too because she said, "I'll get a little paring knife."

"Is it sharp?!"

"Yes."

"Then hurry," Ruff said. "I can almost see the poison spreading."

And he could. Not only were the small child's arm and leg swelling, but there was a dark tinge to her flesh.

Dixie was back in moments with a much smaller knife. Ruff tested it on his thumb and found it to be very sharp. He was shocked to realize that there was a slight tremor in his hands.

"Here," Dixie said, "you help hold Monica still and I'll do this."

Ruff didn't argue. He gripped the child's arm and Dixie seemed to gather herself, and then she sliced Monica's flesh a quarter inch deep. She made a crisscross. The child was already whimpering—now she screamed. Just before Dixie dropped her mouth to the welling wound, Ruff swore he could see a thin, milky-looking fluid that he thought was the snake's venom.

Dixie sucked the wound so hard her cheeks formed deep hollows. Over and over she drew blood and poison from the wound and spat it aside.

"We'd better move to the leg now," Ruff said.

Dixie spat and nodded. "Hold it steady."

Again Dixie made the incisions and tried to remove the venom. Her face was covered with blood and after a minute, Ruff jumped up and retrieved a canteen. "Here, wash your mouth out with this and spit!"

Dixie did.

"Take the child away and I'll do the reverend," Ruff said. "Brother Tucker, hold still now! We've got to do this quick or the poison will already be moving through your body."

"Oh, to hell with *my* body!" Tucker protested. "It's Monica that matters!"

"So do you," Ruff said, jerking up the man's pantsleg to expose the fang marks just above his right ankle.

He used the paring knife and cut deep because the flesh was so thick. The wound bled heavily and Ruff sucked at the wound like a man dying of thirst working on a lemon. The blood, poison, or both tasted salty. It made him feel queasy, but Ruff kept sucking until he was sure that it was useless to continue. Then he ripped his bandanna from his throat and used it to encircle the wound.

The reverend also looked ghastly. "What now?"

Ruff shook his head. He had to be honest with the man. "I don't know. My father taught us how to treat a horse's snakebites, but he also said that a healthy animal almost never died and you mostly had to worry about abscesses, inflammation, and infection."

Reverend Tucker sat up and stared at his bandaged ankle. His expression was one of devastation. He reached out to touch his wife's battered face. Suddenly, he threw his head back and shouted, "Why, Lord! Why!"

Ruff wished the man wouldn't shout at the top of his lungs, because out here on these open Texas plains, sound carried for miles. Also, Ruff wished that he had an answer for the reverend. The man and his darling child were big-hearted, big-souled human beings that deserved better than to die of poisonous snakebites.

Ruff took the canteen from Dixie and, careful to avoid her questioning eyes, he washed out his own mouth.

"What now?" Dixie asked.

"I don't know," Ruff answered. "I guess we just pray. Seems to me that it's in the Lord's hands now."

Dixie swallowed. Taking her own handkerchief and the canteen, she knelt down beside Mrs. Tucker and began to cleanse that nasty gash in her forehead. Dixie mixed her tears with the canteen's water.

NINE

That night the wind came up and it blew hard. The grove of cottonwoods creaked as branches whipped leaves around like green snow. Ruff knew that there would be no risk in building a small campfire because the smoke would be windblown to forever. So, with Monica and the reverend both sick and feverish, they slaughtered the last of their Tucker goats and fed the children their first hot food in days. To everyone's surprise and dismay, the Reverend Tucker declined to eat.

"But you've got to eat," his wife pleaded.

Tucker shook his head. "I feel like I'm burning up inside but I'd gladly roast in hell forever if it would help poor Monica. How is she?"

Across their wind-whipped campfire, Anna, Ruff, and Dixie exchanged guarded glances. When it became clear that Anna could not trust herself to answer, Dixie said, "Monica is holding her own, Reverend. She's doing . . . all right."

The reverend studied his young daughter. Monica was as pale as soda. "She looks awful! Can't we do anything more for her?"

Ruff had repeatedly asked himself the same question. "If we had some whiskey or spirits—"

"No whiskey," Tucker snapped. "No demon rum for my angel girl!"

"Austin ought to have a doctor," Dixie said. "How much farther?"

It was the same question Ruff had been asking himself over and over. He ground his palms into his eyes. "I don't know. I'm guessing seventy or eighty miles."

Dixie touched Monica's cheek, then stood and motioned Ruff outside the circle of fire where she could speak frankly. "Ruff, the child is on fire! Her pulse is over a hundred beats a minute and her respiration is labored. The poison is affecting her heart."

"I know," Ruff said. "Dixie, we just have to accept that there's a good chance that she won't make it."

"But if she could see a doctor . . ."

Ruff stared at his sister. He was worried sick and this talk of doctors made no damn sense. "Say it out plain, Dixie. I've no patience for guessing games."

"I'm saying that that Monica doesn't weigh fifty pounds. You could hold her in front of you and race on to find a doctor in Austin. High Fire could be there by late tomorrow night even if Austin is a hundred miles away."

"And leave all of you behind?" Ruff couldn't believe he was hearing her correctly. Maybe the wind in the trees was playing games with their voices.

"We could stay hidden in this grove," Dixie argued. "The reverend isn't going to be able to handle a team. In three, five days at the most, you'll be back from Austin with help."

Ruff gazed up at the windblown branches tickling the belly of the starry sky. "It's a hard night and a ride like you're talking about might kill the child."

"But if we do nothing, Monica will die for sure. You know that as well as I do. And there's always the chance that Austin is *less* than fifty miles! Ruff, it might be only a few hours south."

"I don't think so. We haven't even crossed the Brazos River yet."

"Ruff, then let *me* take her."

"No!" He lowered his voice. "You wouldn't be strong enough to hold Monica upright that long. And if you tried to lay her across High Fire behind the saddle . . . it'd kill her for certain, Dixie."

"Will you take her, then?" Dixie was pleading.

"I'll give it a little thought," Ruff said, hating the idea of leaving his sister and the others behind and in so much danger.

"There isn't much time," Dixie said. "Ruff, our pa was a gambler. If Monica is to have any chance at all of surviving this, we've got to take a big gamble right now!"

Ruff pulled away from his sister and went back to sit cross-legged beside the feverish child. He realized that Anna Tucker was staring at him.

"What were you and Dixie talking about just now?" the woman asked. "Was it about Monica and my husband?"

"Yes, ma'am."

When Ruff lowered his eyes to the flames, Dixie said, "We were discussing trying to get Monica to a doctor in Austin. Ruff could support her in the saddle. High Fire is still strong and I believe Ruff could get your daughter to a doctor in Austin by late tomorrow night. It might be her only chance."

"Then do it!" the woman cried passionately. "Please, do it!"

Ruff took Monica's pulse. It was beating like the wings of a hummingbird. Her breathing was rapid and shallow. He made up his mind. "I'll saddle High Fire. Get Monica ready for the night ride as best you can. I'll leave at once."

Dixie and the woman jumped to their feet and began to bustle around. Reverend Tucker mumbled something but drifted back into a restless sleep. Ruff grabbed his saddle and bridle. High Fire was young and he was strong. Well, tonight he was going to make the run of his life. Ruff just hoped that this wasn't a fool's errand. And if Monica died en route and this camp were attacked by Comanche before he could return . . .

Ruff pushed that nightmarish thought out of his mind. It was too terrible to even contemplate. Dixie was all that he had left. Houston was somewhere up in the North, probably dead by now or locked up in some federal prison for the duration of the Civil War. Dixie and he were all that were really left for sure of the once-renowned horsemen known as the Ballou family. And if he lost his kid sister Ruff didn't know what he'd do. With that thought in mind, not only did he saddle High Fire, but he saddled old High Man. If this camp were attacked and there was no hope of saving themselves, he wanted Dixie to have a chance.

"Monica is ready," Dixie said, coming upon him by the picket line, "and . . . what are you saddling High Man for?"

"Figure it out," Ruff snapped, feeling miserable for what he was about to demand of his sister. "I want you to keep this horse saddled and *use* him if it comes down to a choice between runnin'—or dyin'."

Dixie's eyes widened. "You mean . . ."

"Getting yourself killed wouldn't help any of them," Ruff gritted. "And they'd understand."

"But I'd never forgive myself! And if the situation were reversed, you'd never run out on them, either."

Ruff whirled on his sister and grabbed her by the arms. "Listen to me! If there's no other chance to save yourself, *you take this one!* Otherwise, I'm staying."

Dixie began to tremble. She struggled to speak. "I'm not sure that I could, Ruff."

Ruff released her. He felt awful even talking about this but it was something that had to be understood between them. "All right, if it would make it any easier, take the Tuckers' infant and both of you skedaddle. Could you at least do that much if the Comanche find and attack you in numbers too large to hold off until I return?"

Dixie slowly nodded her head. "Yes. I could do that."

Ruff expelled a deep breath and released his sister. "Let's just hope it isn't necessary. In the morning, eat a quick breakfast and then kill the fire and keep it dead until I return. If I don't return, stay until the reverend can drive, and then hurry south, traveling only at night."

"All right." Dixie threw her arms around her brother. *"You* be careful, too!"

"Don't worry about me," Ruff said as he finished saddling his own horse. "High Fire can outrun anything on these Texas plains except antelope. And he'd even run them into the ground after a couple of miles."

"Well," Dixie said, "you just keep running until you reach Austin."

"Count on it," Ruff promised, leading his handsome young Thoroughbred over to their campfire and the feverish Monica Tucker.

When Ruff started to lift the child, she suddenly came awake and began to thrash with demented fury. "It's all right, child," Ruff soothed. "It's all right."

Reverend Tucker's eyes flew open. He struggled for clarity of mind. "What . . ."

"Go back to sleep, my darling," Anna said, dropping to her husband's side. "Everything will be just fine."

Tucker's lips moved and with his face bathed in the dancing flames of their campfire, it suddenly struck Ruff just how much weight the man had lost since leaving the little Cherokee town of Saugus. Just three weeks ago, the reverend had been a horse of a man, with round appled cheeks and a huge girth. Now he looked old and shaky. His cheeks were waxen and hollowed. His once-expansive waistline had melted away.

"The Lord will provide," Tucker whispered.

"Of course he will," Anna said, lifting her husband's head to be cradled in her lap.

Anna looked up at Ruff as he placed Monica in his saddle, then stepped up and squeezed his rump into the saddle behind her. It was going to be a tight fit but there was no other way to hold Monica across the long miles they were about to travel.

"Go with God, Brother Ballou!" the woman whispered fervently. "Fly on the wings of angels!"

Ruff screwed his hat down tight and looked to Dixie. "You know what to do if you must," he said simply.

"Good-bye." Dixie tightened the bandages on Monica's arm and leg. "And good luck."

"We'll make it and we'll save this child," Rufff vowed as he wheeled the tall, sorrel horse away from the fire and sent it plunging out of the dark, wind-punished woods. Out in the open, his hat was immediately torn from his head and went sailing off toward the cold moon.

To hell with it, Ruff thought as he turned his back on the North Star and sent the stallion galloping forward into the swirling wind and the moonlight.

It was a devilish night with the moon and stars brighter than Ruff had ever seen and the wind gusting and howling like wild witches. Heavy black clouds sailed across the moon and distant thunder echoed over the grasslands like vengeful, ancient gods making war.

To Ruff's great relief, Monica Tucker lost consciousness almost immediately. High Fire was not rested but the stallion was willing. Ruff gave the Thoroughbred free rein until he could feel the animal's stride begin to shorten and then he pulled the stallion into a walk, then later a trot and finally, a gallop again. He judged that they were making a steady ten miles an hour and thought they could sustain that pace through both the night and the following day.

Sometime after midnight, he was heartened to see silver ribbon winding across the land and knew he had at last come upon the Brazos River. Ruff trotted to its northern bank and let High Fire drink his fill before he prodded the horse into the water and crossed. The Brazos was much easier to ford than the Red River, and when it had been forded, Ruff dismounted and carried Monica over to a small, grassy place along the riverbank.

Her pulse was still racing and her skin was hot to the touch. Because of the wind, he had trouble guessing her rate of breathing, but it was still dangerously fast.

"Just don't give up on us," Ruff pleaded, staring at the child's pale, innocent face.

In contrast to his own raging emotions, Monica looked very much at peace, but that gave Ruff no comfort. While High Fire grazed on the banks of the Brazos, Ruff recounted this child's many delightful moods and poses. How she'd loved to explore and climb trees and how she had such a fiery temper and insisted on standing up to her older brothers whenever her rights seemed to have been infringed upon.

Ruff forced himself to remain beside the Brazos because High Fire needed time to graze and Ruff was desperate for a few minutes of sleep. And so, unbidden, he dozed by the river and when he awoke, the eastern horizon was ablaze with the rising orb of fire.

Ruff shook his head and his first impulse was to look down at Monica, still cradled in his arms. The child yet lived. A miracle. Feeling drugged rather than refreshed, Ruff staggered to his feet. He trudged over to his stallion, tightened his cinch, and then lifted Monica back into his saddle.

"I'm sorry I didn't even remove your bridle so you could eat better," he told the stallion.

High Fire nickered softly and Ruff allowed himself a moment to scratch the horse behind the ears. Then he booted his stirrup and said, "Let's go find Austin!"

The four-year-old Ballou stallion lifted into an easy gallop. Ruff held the child tight and kept his eyes drilled to the south. Maybe that's why he did not see the Comanche until it was much too late.

TEN

The instant that Ruff saw the huge Comanche hunting party, his veins flooded with ice water and his heart felt as if it were caught in the iron jaws of a mighty vise. The Comanche were only about a quarter of a mile south, between him and Austin. Ruff drew High Fire to a standstill because the tall Thoroughbred had been galloping for the last fifteen minutes and he was breathing heavily.

Time stood still. The Comanche were surprised to see a lone and therefore vulnerable horseman on their empty prairie. They too drew in their mounts. There were at least thirty warriors, most of whom were armed with rifles. They weren't painted nor were they wearing big warbonnets or anything so fancy, but even at a distance they looked fierce.

Ruff squeezed the unconscious Monica Tucker to his chest and his mind reeled off his precious few options. Even as he watched, the Comanche began to fan out and walk their horses forward in a long line that effectively blocked him from reaching help to the south. Ruff knew that he couldn't retrace his steps north to the Tucker camp. He'd be damned it he'd contribute to the deaths of the Tucker family and poor Dixie.

That left him only the options of fleeing either to the east or west. If he ran west, he'd be racing into the unknown, and every mile would carry him farther away from any hope of reaching a town or army fort. Even as he narrowed his choice down to the east, High Fire trumpeted a challenge to the Comanche horses, several of whom answered. The stallion pawed the earth, suddenly revitalized with the prospect of meeting other horses. Its spirit proved inspirational to Ruff and it calmed him. He stroked the young stallion's neck.

It was, he thought, a pity that High Fire was already very tired and out of breath for, otherwise, they'd have had a very interesting horse race with the stakes being life or death. As it was, Ruff had no doubt that the Comanche knew that he was riding a played-out horse because they could easily see that the Thoroughbred was covered with sweat and heavily lathered.

"I'm sorry," Ruff said, buying each precious second to allow his horse to catch its wind, "but we're going to have to run for our lives."

Ruff slowly reined High Fire to the west. Then, he began to walk away from the line of approaching Indians, still buying his weary Thoroughbred precious moments to slow his pulse and breathing.

The Comanche were surprised by the lone horseman's measured reaction to their advance. They pushed their ponies into an easy jog, and when Ruff was forced to match that pace, the Comanche kicked their ponies into an easy but determined lope.

"Here we go," Ruff said.

High Fire, however, was very interested in the Comanche horses and kept rolling his eyes around, trying to watch them come at him. The stallion sensed Ruff's apprehension but didn't understand it. To him, these were just people and horses, and perhaps there would even be a horse race coming or . . . far better, a mare to breed. Such was the magnificent Thoroughbred's only experience around large groups of strange horses.

High Fire reluctantly moved into a long, swinging canter that appeared relaxed and even slow, but was, in fact, deceptively fast because of the tremendous length of his stride. The Comanche, expert horsemen by any account, were fooled for a few seconds by High Fire's easy, fluid movement, but very quickly they realized that their quarry was fast outdistancing them.

Ruff heard a howl of anger and then a shot. He twisted around in his saddle and saw that the Comanche had already tired of their game and were pushing their horses into a hard run.

"Let's show them what a Ballou horse can do," Ruff said, asking High Fire to really run.

The stallion laid back its ears and even though it was bone weary, it began to extend its magnificent stride, legs flying out and gobbling up the earth in a way that amazed the Comanche, who howled even louder. Ruff heard more shots and thought that he heard the sound of lead whistling past his ears, but he couldn't be sure. High Fire galloped for ten minutes, not quite as hard as if he were in a tough race with Thoroughbreds nearly his equal, but fast enough to extend the distance and carry Ruff and Monica out of rifle range. The Comanche were angling off to the southwest so that Ruff had no hope of flanking them to reach Austin. As Ruff pulled the stallion down to a trot, his heart sank to note how his horse was already a little shaky on his feet.

Glancing over his shoulder, Ruff saw that the Comanche were still galloping and dissolving the distance Ruff had just put between himself and the Indians. Ruff beat back a rising panic. These were the first real Plains Indians he had ever encountered and they were demonstrating that they were superior horsemen and that their mounts were in excellent condition. What their ponies lacked in pure, blazing speed they easily made up for with their incredible endurance. Ruff knew that they'd overtake him sooner rather than later.

"I'm sorry," Ruff said to his horse as he forced High Fire back into a weary lope, "but we're out of choices."

Ruff mentally counted pounds and knew that High Fire was carrying about a hundred more than the Indian ponies. He came to that figure because he was taller and heavier than the Indians and his saddle outweighed theirs by a good thirty pounds. Add that to Monica's weight and it was easy to calculate the failing Thoroughbred's extra burden.

Even that might not have been a fatal disadvantage. What was going to prove Ruff's certain undoing was the fact that High Fire had been running on and off all night and was practically dead on his feet. Another few miles and the stallion's wind would break or he'd just be unable to run any farther.

Ruff could see far into the distance and there was nothing ahead of him but rolling hills, a few stands of forest, and oceans of grass. He wasn't going to get out of this one alive. All he could hope was that the Comanche would kill him quickly and do the same to the child he cradled in the crook of his left arm. Ruff took no comfort that the Tucker child was probably going to die of her snakebites anyway.

He fixed his eyes on a stand of trees several miles distant. If he could reach them, then he would sell his life a little more dearly. He'd use his rifle and then his six-shot pistols until he was finished. Maybe he would save the last two bullets for the child and for himself. Ruff didn't know if he could do that but, like most people, he'd heard terrible and gruesome stories of Indian tortures.

Ruff twisted around in his saddle and he saw that a few of the Comanche riding the fastest horses had detached themselves from the main body of horsemen and were closing the gap.

"Come on!" Ruff whispered to his flagging Thoroughbred. "Just get us to those trees."

But try as he might, High Fire was shot. His every breath made a tearing sound in his gullet and it broke Ruff's heart to think of how the gallant stallion was literally dying between his legs trying to carry him to . . . to what? A stand of trees where he would, at best, only manage to drop a few more Indians before they killed him?

Something in Ruff rebelled at the cruelty of ruining the stallion who was fighting to run even as his stride was breaking apart like a cheap toy. Then a cry flooded Ruff's throat as High Fire's nostrils began to spew bloody spray. Ruff drew the valiant animal to a standstill, and it almost collapsed as he jumped to the earth, yanked his rifle from its scabbard, then laid the feverish child down on the grass and moving aside to take a prone firing position.

Ruff took aim at the lead Comanche but just as he pulled the trigger of his single-shot rifle, the Indian seemed to anticipate the shot. He jerked his reins hard to the right and the horse was caught accidentally by Ruff's bullet. The animal collapsed into a rolling dive and the Comanche was thrown over its head. He struck the grass and skidded to a twitching halt. He tried to get up but could not. The other Comanche fired at Ruff and then veered off to both sides and swept out of rifle range as Ruff drew his six-gun.

The injured Comanche was bleeding from his ears and Ruff guessed that the man had suffered a concussion. He was confused and in a great deal of pain. Ruff raised his pistol and drew a bead on the Indian's head thinking he would at least be guaranteed the satisfaction of taking one Comanche with him into eternity. But the fallen warrior, hearing the cocking of the six-gun, turned his head toward Ruff and began his death chant. Ruff just couldn't find it in himself to pull the trigger. The injured warrior was no longer a threat.

The only thought that comforted Ruff was in knowing that little Monica would never know when the end arrived. Ruff had always thought he would die on a Civil War battlefield beside friends and maybe his brothers, but never on the Texas plains with a poisoned child and a confused and badly injured Comanche warrior.

The Comanche had drawn up their horses and watched him with hard, confident faces. They did, however, seem a little confused as to why he hadn't put a bullet through the downed warrior. Ruff saw a knot of the apparent leaders rein their horses together in a lively conversation. They kept pointing at Ruff and their fallen companion.

Ruff stood up and went over to wait beside High Fire. The stallion's head was hanging low as it struggled for breath and trembled. Ruff reached under the jaw and took the Thoroughbred's pulse. It was just under a hundred and falling. Ruff looked into the suffering animal's eyes and he saw no signs that the horse was in shock. There was no outpouring of blood from the nostrils so that meant the lungs were not hemorrhaging.

"You're going to make it," he said to the beaten animal. "You're probably going to become a Comanche horse and have lots and lots of Indian mares to breed. You'll be prized beyond measure when they realize that the size of your heart matches your incredible speed."

Ruff turned to watch the Comanche, who had begun to encircle him. There was no hope of escape. But then, there never had been, given the Thoroughbred's exhausted condition.

Ruff yanked on his latigo and uncinched High Fire. He carried his saddle a few feet from child and horse. He tipped the saddle on edge and removed an extra Colt from his saddlebags. The morning sun glared meanly into his face and he had no hat so Ruff edged around a little until he was facing south. Then he laid his Colts out behind the saddle and prepared to make a good accounting of the last few seconds of his short, exciting life. There wasn't a single doubt in Ruff's nineteen-year-old mind that he was about to meet the Lord as well as Justin, his father, and his brothers Micha, John, and Mason.

But the Comanche did not swarm and overrun him. Instead, they watched. Finally, one warrior separated from the others and rode toward Ruff and the fallen warrior, rifle butt resting on his thigh, chin up, eyes and hair blacker than Ruff's. He was riding a pinto stallion that began to challenge High Man in voice and head movement. The Comanche chief rode an Indian saddle that was little more than a pair of stirrups tied to a leather pad. The reins he held in his left hand were rawhide and the stallion was controlled by nothing more than a length of rawhide through its mouth. Ruff found himself admiring the horse as well as its master, who rode as if he'd been born on horseback.

When the rider drew near to the fallen Comanche, he reined his pinto to a dancing halt, then slipped off the horse. For a moment, his and Ruff's eyes locked, and then the chief looked down at his fallen tribesman and then back to Ruff.

"Go ahead and take him," Ruff said, "I won't shoot you until you come shooting at me."

"Long Bow hurt."

Ruff was surprised that the Comanche spoke English but he supposed he shouldn't have been. If an Indian carried a rifle, he'd have had to trade for it with whites. As his Comanche father might have traded for rifles, steel knives, and such things from the earlier fur traders and trappers.

The chief turned his back on Ruff and paused, displaying great bravery to his people. He was not afraid of death. When Ruff did not shoot, the chief finally motioned his companions forward. Four of them came, and when they reached Long Bow, they also dismounted and examined the injured warrior. After several minutes of consultation, they picked him up and carried him away, leaving his dead horse behind.

The first warrior now regarded Ruff with as much interest as hostility. "Comanche!" he grunted, whacking his buckskin-clad chest.

"Cherokee!" Ruff called, then also pounded his breast with doubled fist.

"Cherokee?"

"Uh-huh. Mixed blood."

The warrior looked over his shoulder to see if the others had heard. Their expressions showed that they had. The chief pointed at Monica Tucker. "What wrong?"

"Snakebite. Very bad. I was trying to reach white medicine man in Austin."

"Hmmph!" the warrior grunted.

Ruff didn't know how to reply to that so he knelt beside the girl, rifle cradled across his bended knee, both six-guns close at hand. As far as he was concerned, what happened next was up to the Comanche.

The warrior whose horse Ruff had shot seemed to be recovering a little. He was now on his feet, though bent over, cradling his head and still obviously in a great deal of pain.

"I am Buffalo Killer," the Comanche announced.

"I am Rufus Ballou."

"Cherokee name?"

"Ruff."

"Ruff?" the warrior repeated, as if the word had a strange taste.

"Yes."

Buffalo Killer shrugged. "Girl's name?"

"Monica Tucker. She is also part Cherokee."

Buffalo's eyebrows lifted and it was clear that he didn't believe that. "Red hair, pale face."

"Part Cherokee," Ruff quickly added. "Maybe not much."

Buffalo turned and called out something. Immediately, an older man with bowed legs and a leather bag draped across one shoulder who had been attending the dazed warrior detached from the others and came forward. He spoke to Buffalo for a moment and then came over to kneel beside Monica without even looking at Ruff.

"Snakebite," Ruff said, reaching out to take Monica's pulse and finding it to be very fast. Her skin was still on fire.

The man who examined Monica left little doubt that he was a medicine man when he opened his leather pouch and examined its contents, then began to speak rapidly to Buffalo Killer. After several minutes, Buffalo issued a command and more Comanche came forward. They reeked of smoke, horse, and sweat. They were considerably shorter than Ruff, all boasting prominent cheekbones and strong features. They were handsome and moved with the smoothness of flowing water.

A fire was quickly built and a kettle was found on one of the Indian pack ponies. Water was set to boil and Buffalo Killer sat down cross-legged near the girl, causing most of the other Comanche to do the same.

The medicine man began to chant and dance near his smoking kettle while a couple of Indians fed the fire with buffalo chips and sticks.

"What's he going to do?" Ruff asked.

The chief, who was probably in his late twenties, looked through Ruff without answering. Maybe, Ruff decided, the man thought the question unworthy of a reply. For whatever reason, nothing more was said and Ruff didn't ask any more questions. He just squatted on the grass beside his stallion as it slowly recovered and then began to graze.

Buffalo Killer's sorrel stallion edged over and bit High Fire. The Thoroughbred was taller but lighter boned and not as heavily coupled. When High Fire bit back, both stallions squealed and would have gone for the legs or necks but the Comanche jumped in between them and forced them off in different directions.

Ruff stayed with his guns, though it was obvious that they were all but useless now in such close quarters, surrounded by forty or fifty warriors. And when the medicine man began to add leaves and other things from his medicine pouch to the water, Ruff saw that the man was preparing a poultice.

Ruff did not hold much with Indian medicines. Even the Cherokee up in the Indian Territory had all but abandoned it in favor of the white man's medicine. However, there were still some natural herbs and medicines that the whites did not use but were still very useful. Ruff hoped that the Comanche medicine man carried a miracle in his leather pouch for Monica Tucker.

When the first steaming poultice was pressed to the snakebites, Monica cried out from the depths of her fevered existence. She thrashed and had to be restrained. Quickly, however, the poultice cooled and when it was removed, Ruff saw that the snakebite wounds were dark purple and looked very infected. Up until then, they had been covered by bandages.

Again and again the poultices were laid to rest on Monica's inflamed flesh until the child was bathed in sweat and torment.

"Hasn't she had enough?" Ruff demanded.

"Comanche medicine strong!" Buffalo said.

Ruff had no reply. He indicated to the chief that he wanted to ride High Fire down to a nearby stream so that the horse could drink. Ruff knew the animal was dehydrated because when he pinched High Fire's flesh, it stayed puckered. That meant that the animal had no moisture in its body, which was no small wonder considering how long and hard it had run since the last time he had found water.

Buffalo Killer indicated to Ruff that he could walk High Fire over to the stream but he was not to mount the horse.

"Don't worry," Ruff said, "I wouldn't run out on Monica."

Buffalo Killer seemed to understand either the words or the indignant tone of Ruff's voice. Whichever it was, he nodded.

The stream was a mile distant and Ruff half expected to be shot in the back for the first few hundred yards. But he wasn't, and when they arrived at the stream, he let the stallion have his fill because the horse was now well cooled down.

"You're going to be fine," Ruff said, scratching High Fire behind the ears. "I don't know what's going to become of Monica or me, but I know without a doubt that you've impressed the hell out of these Indians. Maybe they'll all kill each other off fighting over you. By then, those poultices will have done their good work and the child's fever will have been broken and the poisoning run its course. In that case, we'll just rejoin her folks and all go on to Austin to live happily every after."

The stallion paid Ruff no mind as he talked nonsense. When it had drunk its fill, Ruff led High Fire back to the Comanche. Most of the warriors came over to admire the young Thoroughbred who was already perking up nicely.

Ruff repeated the animal's name to them many times. The Comanche actually smiled and Ruff suspected it was because they were picturing him dead and them proudly owning this fine specimen of horseflesh. He didn't know that for a fact, but it certainly made for interesting speculation.

ELEVEN

Ruff and Buffalo Killer sat beside the campfire that night watching the medicine man attend to Monica Tucker. The other Comanche mostly gathered around the fire as well, although some preferred to sleep among their prized buffalo ponies.

They had feasted on buffalo hump and when Ruff had asked the Comanche chief where he had managed to find the buffalo, the man had declined to answer. Once, however, Buffalo Killer had turned to Ruff and surprised him with a most unexpected question.

"Do the Cherokee believe this land was given to the Indian peoples?"

By luck or coincidence, it was one of the few Cherokee legends that Ruff remembered being told by his mother while still a small child. "A long time ago the Cherokee say that the land was covered with water. The Great Buzzard, the father of all birds, flew for a long, long time over the water seeking a place to land. He flew for so many moons that his great wings fanned the waters until they dried up and became mud."

Ruff paused. The Comanche were very interested in his story and were looking at him as if he finally had something important to say. Ruff stared into the flames and remembered himself as a boy, listening to this ancient Cherokee story. For the first time in many years, he could almost see his beautiful Cherokee mother lost to a cholera epidemic when he was twelve years old.

"When the water was changed to mud, the Great Buzzard hoped to find dry land where he could rest, but there was nothing yet but mud. He grew very, very tired. His great wings became so heavy that their tips began to strike the earth. The Great Buzzard tried to fly higher, and so hard did he beat his huge wings that when he raised them up, the mud underneath lifted to become mountains. And wherever the tips of his wings touched the mud, he created valleys."

"And what about *this* land?" a Comanche wanted to know.

Ruff realized that he had to say something flattering about these vast Texas plains. "This land of the Comanche the Great Buzzard found most to his liking. As he landed, his great wings swept this land smooth. It is here that he would call his home."

The Comanche were delighted with the outcome of this Cherokee legend. They did not the least bit suspect Ruff had altered it to gain their satisfaction.

"And what of your people?" Ruff dared to ask.

"We believe that the Great Spirit created this land for the Indian," Buffalo Killer said. "But at first, there was no buffalo and the People were always hungry. Finally, one day a brave warrior went far away and he discovered a hole in the earth. Going inside, he found the buffalo and stampeded them across the land. Before horse came to the People, the buffalo were hard to kill, for they had great power. They spoke to Earth, the mother of all living things, by pawing or throwing it up with their horns. The Comanche speak to Earth by our prayers but also by painting ourselves with her clays."

"I see. And when the buffalo are no more?"

"Then the People will be no more." Buffalo Killer came to his feet and moved out among the horses, telling Ruff more plainly than words that he did not wish any more conversation.

Ruff did not sleep well among the Comanche that night. It was not so much that he expected that these people would murder him in his sleep, but that he felt responsible for Monica and tried to stay aware of what the medicine man was doing to break her fever and cleanse her of the snake's venom.

The medicine man relied heavily upon his steaming poultices but it was obvious that his chants and rituals with smoke, beads, and feathers were also very important. Ruff knew that the early full-blood Cherokee also had their chants, dances, and special ceremonies, but that part of his Indian heritage had long ago vanished among the Cherokee. For more than a century the Cherokee had eagerly adopted the white man's ways, even to drawing up a constitution based on that of the United States of America. However, to their great misfortune, the white man's ways had only brought the Cherokee scorn and a forced relocation to the West.

In contrast to the Cherokee, it was clear to Ruff that these Comanche had compromised nothing of their traditional life-style or values. And even though the great herds of buffalo were almost gone, the Comanche still were nomadic and because of this were considered to be "hostiles" by the United States government because they would not confine themselves to a reservation. Also, the Comanche, Kiowa, and other hostile Indian tribes made war not only on whites, but on the settled reservation Indians, whom they held with great contempt.

Ruff had never seen such fierce Indians and wondered if, long before his own ancestors had intermarried and then tried to adopt the white man's life-style, if they had also been so bold and warlike. Ruff supposed that they had been, but he could not be certain.

One other thing that had kept Ruff awake that night was his concern for the welfare of the Tucker family and his sister, Dixie. By now, they would expect him to be in Austin getting medical attention for Monica. They would be praying for his speedy return, perhaps even with a United States Army or Texas Ranger patrol for escort. But days would pass and then they would accept the fact that no help was coming. When they could wait no longer, they would follow High Fire's hoofprints south. And, unless things changed, they would blunder into this Comanche war party.

Ruff's mind was in turmoil for he could think of no way to warn Dixie and the Tuckers. And he fretted that Moody Tucker himself might die of snake poison even as the medicine man was saving Monica's life. Several times that night, Ruff had a powerful impulse to sneak over to High Fire and vault onto the Thoroughbred's back, then race away. But each time reason prevailed. Where could he run? Not to the Tuckers because he would be followed by these warriors. And furthermore, he could not abandon the little girl, even though it was becoming apparent that the Comanche would do her no harm.

What, Ruff wondered, if he just confessed to Buffalo Killer that he had left his sister and the Tucker family in an attempt to reach Austin and a doctor? Would the chief then order his warriors to go kill those people, Dixie included? Ruff didn't know. Over and over he asked himself if this was the same hunting party that had kidnapped the boy whose toys he and the reverend had found. Ruff finally decided that he could not risk telling Buffalo Killer anything until he knew more about him and this hunting party. If these Comanche were the ones that had pinned the kidnapped child's parents to the earth, then they would probably do the same to the Tuckers and to Dixie.

With daybreak came the warming sun and to Ruff's great joy, Monica opened her eyes and they were clear. The medicine man, whose name was Calling Hawk, was very proud of the results of his labors. He threw his head back and shouted in triumph as the other Comanche grinned proudly.

When Monica's eyes widened with fear and she started to cry, Ruff hurried to her side. "It's all right," he said, "everything is all right."

"Where's Mommy and Daddy!"

Ruff groaned and tried to press his hand over the child's mouth but it was too late. He could see Buffalo Killer looking right into his eyes, waiting. Ruff let the Comanche chief wait. He decided that he would not tell Buffalo Killer of the whereabouts of Dixie and the rest of the Tucker family.

But it didn't matter. That morning when the Indians broke camp, they begin to follow Ruff's trail back toward the Brazos River. When they came to it, they rested and took a nap while their ponies grazed. Two hours later, they were on horseback again. Monica rode double with Ruff just as she'd done while unconscious. Long Bow, the man whose pony Ruff had accidentally killed, rode double with another Comanche. Long Bow was still suffering from his fall and resulting concussion. He would shake his head and sometimes squeeze it with both hands. Once or twice, he would groan and all that day, Ruff caught the Indian staring at him with murder in his obsidian eyes.

Ruff knew that the warrior felt humiliated and that he was filled with pain and hate for the man who'd shot his horse and caused him a grievous injury. Ruff made a mental note to keep his eyes on Long Bow and not turn his back on the warrior for a single second. Long Bow had a pistol jammed under his belt, and every time their eyes met, Ruff expected the Indian to use it. If that happened, Ruff was not sure what he would do. The Comanche had not disarmed him but it was made clear that if he used his guns he would die.

Ruff said a silent prayer that Long Bow had enough reason left in his battered brain not to go for his pistol. If he did, Ruff knew that he was a dead man one way or the other.

Even more pressing than his own safety was the realization that High Fire's tracks were leading them straight to the Tucker family camp and there wasn't a damn thing that Ruff could do or say to change the fact. If he tried, his ruse would be pathetically obvious and incur among the Comanche the loss of some small measure of respect he seemed to have earned.

Late that afternoon they camped near a spring that gurgled sweetly out of the earth, creating a vast marsh before it vanished again into the prairie. Ruff accepted a pair of rawhide hobbles from the Comanche and put High Fire out to graze. He started to turn away when he heard an angry squeal and then a stallion's trumpeted challenge. Ruff whipped around just in time to see Buffalo Killer's big pinto stallion rush High Fire. The pinto was not hobbled and it came at High Fire like a locomotive, ears back flat, nostrils flaring, big yellow teeth going for the Thoroughbred's neck.

Ruff shouted and started to leap forward to help his horse in any way he could, including shooting the damned pinto who had the great advantage of having its front legs free of hobbles. But two warriors jumped into Ruff's path with drawn knives. The pinto hit High Fire with its shoulder, knocking the Thoroughbred over. Ruff knew that the pinto stallion would stomp his horse to death before High Fire could get to his feet.

Ruff understood the consequences of any action he took against the Comanche but he was so enraged by the injustice of the contest between the stallions that he didn't give a damn. Charging forward, he lashed out with a boot and kicked one of the Indians in the forearm, knocking the man's knife spinning. The other Comanche cursed and jumped at Ruff, knife coming in low and quick. Ruff stabbed out with his hand and tried to grab the Comanche's wrist. He missed but did succeed in deflecting the blow that would have gutted him.

Ruff smashed the second Comanche with a chopping left hook and then caught him on the side of the face with a wild, looping uppercut. The second Comanche crashed over backward but the first threw himself on Ruff, locking an arm around his throat. Ruff saw High Fire struggling to get up even as the pinto stallion's sharp hooves came down on his side. When the hooves struck, it sounded like the hollow boom of a drum. High Fire's teeth snapped on the pinto's leg and he held on for dear life as the Comanche tried to throttle Ruff.

Ruff slammed his elbow backward into the Comanche's stomach. He heard the warrior grunt, and that gave Ruff all the encouragement he needed to pound the man three more times in the gut, each blow wicked enough to lift the Indian completely off his feet. But the tenacious Comanche would not break his hold.

Ruff stomped the heel of his boot down on the Comanche's moccasin. The Indian howled and lost his choke hold. Ruff battered the man twice, breaking his nose and loosening teeth.

The Comanche's eyes rolled up in his head. Ruff started to jump up but the first Indian kicked him in the ribs and sent him sprawling. Lying on his back, gasping, Ruff saw the Indian leap high in the air with the intention of landing on his chest with doubled knees. Ruff rolled sideways, heard the Indian strike the earth, then he threw himself onto of the warrior. Ruff grabbed the Comanche's long black hair and could have snapped his neck, only he knew that would be his own death warrant, so he simply hit the man behind the ear, knocking him out cold.

Lungs on fire, legs shaky, Ruff threw himself at the pinto stallion. He struck the animal just as it was rearing up to come down on High Fire. Ruff slammed his shoulder into the pinto's haunches with enough driving power in his legs to knock the animal off balance. The pinto crashed to the earth and Ruff ripped off his shirt and attacked it, whipping the pinto with his shirt and yelling into its face.

The pinto stallion scrambled to its feet and galloped away. Ruff knelt beside his High Fire. The Thoroughbred was bleeding in three or four places and its fetlocks were torn from trying to break the hobbles. Ruff drew his own knife and cut the hobbles. The Thoroughbred jumped to its feet and stood trembling.

"Easy," Ruff crooned, hands moving swiftly and reasurringly across the violated hide. "Easy. It's over now, boy."

Ruff began to talk to his badly shaken stallion, calming it with the same mix of Cherokee and English that his father had used as long as Ruff could remember. The two warriors who'd tried to knife Ruff were helped to their feet, and as soon as they had regained their senses, they began to make a big pretense of trying to break free of their companions and attack again.

"This time," Ruff said as much to the stallion as to himself, "if they come at me I'll drop them both with bullets."

Buffalo Killer had not moved during any of the trouble, but now he went over to the two warriors that Ruff had battered and when he spoke to them in his own tongue, Buffalo

Killer's tone was hard and cutting. The pair immediately turned away but not before they glared at Ruff and raised their knives in an unmistakable challenge. Well, Ruff thought as he went to comfort the frightened Tucker child, that makes three that intend to cut out my gizzard and feed it to the coyotes.

That evening around the campfire they finished the delicious buffalo hump. Ruff made a big show of using his bowie knife so that the pair who'd laid down the challenge to kill him would understand that he'd use more than his fists the next time around. When the hour grew late, Ruff took his saddle in one hand and Monica in the other. He figured on leaving the campfire and sleeping out on the plains, where he felt safer and better able to protect Monica, but Buffalo Killer grabbed his arm, pointed to a sleeping place near his own buffalo robe, and said, "Here, Ruff. Girl, too."

When Ruff raised his eyebrows in question, the Comanche chief drew a forefinger across his throat and made a choking sound. Ruff understood. He laid his blanket down for Monica to sleep between himself and the Comanche chief. And even though he tried to stay awake and watchful of his enemies, he fell asleep almost the moment his head was laid to rest on his saddle.

They all slept until well after daybreak. They had some dried pemmican and some soda biscuits that Ruff hoped had not been made by the poor woman he and the reverend had buried. In no apparent hurry, the Comanche finally mounted their horses. High Fire, as Ruff had feared, was stiff and sore. He limped but not badly enough to slow the group down, and after a few miles, the battered Thoroughbred limbered up and traveled along just fine. It did not escape Ruff's attention that the Thoroughbred kept an eye on the pinto stallion at all times. Just as Ruff kept a vigilant eye on the three warriors who planned to skewer him at the very first opportunity.

Earlier that morning, he'd made the Tucker child promise not to mention her parents but he wasn't sure she'd understood a word he'd tried to convey. So Ruff talked to her constantly.

"What is your favorite color?"

"Green," she replied.

"That's a pretty color. Do you like it best because of the trees and the grass?"

"Yes."

"And what is your favorite animal?"

"A dog," she told him. Tears sprang to her eyes. "All our dogs drowned in the river but Daddy promised we'll get new ones in Austin. What's your favorite animal, Ruff?"

"The horse," he said without an instant of hesitation. "You see, horses are God's most beautiful creatures. If well treated and loved, they spend their entire lives trying to help us. They pull wagons and carry us wherever we want to ride. They don't ask for much, they can get by just fine on nothing but grass, and when they run, they make you feel as if you are flying."

"My father doesn't like horses," Monica confessed.

Buffalo Killer turned and looked through Ruff. He seemed to wait for a moment, almost as if he expected Ruff to say something. When Ruff did not, he finally looked away.

"What," Ruff asked, "is your favorite . . . oh, day?"

"Sunday, when my father preaches to the Lord," Monica said.

Ruff gulped, felt Buffalo Killer's eyes boring into the back of his head. "My favorite day," Ruff said quickly, "is the one I'm living."

Buffalo Killer rode out ahead and Ruff thought he knew why.

By noon, Ruff could just distinguish the grove of cotton-wood trees where the Tucker family along with Dixie were camped. Ruff was sweating although the day was cool, the wind brisk and refreshing. His mind kept seeking a way to warn the Tuckers of the approaching Comanche hunting party. Finally, Ruff decided that before the Comanche sighted the Tuckers he should make a break for the grove. High Fire, though battered and sore, was plenty capable of carrying him and Monica to the grove of trees several hundred yards in front of the Comanche if he were not brought down in a hail of Comanche bullets.

But the more that Ruff thought about that, the more he realized that it was a suicidal plan. There were simply too many Comanche and no matter how valiant a stand he, Dixie, and the Tuckers could mount, they would be overrun and slaughtered.

But if they weren't going to fight, that left only one option, and that was to ask Buffalo Killer to spare his sister and the Tucker family from harm. Decision made, Ruff started to draw his horse up but at that very instant, one of the Comanche shouted something and all the others drew up their horses and raised their weapons at arm's length, faces split into wide grins, excited yips and howls pouring from their throats.

Ruff turned and followed their eyes. That's when he saw Dixie running after little two-year-old Rachel Tucker. Dixie caught the toddler and looked up to see the Comanche. The distance was almost a half mile, but Ruff thought he could sense Dixie's panic and terror at the sight of the huge number of Comanche. She scooped up Rachel and dashed back into the grove of cottonwoods.

Buffalo Killer's head swiveled around and he pinned Ruff with his black, accusing eyes. He didn't have to say a word.

"The girl is my sister and the little one is this child's youngest sister," Ruff blurted, looking down at Monica. "They are all part Indian. Part Cherokee."

Time seemed to stand still as Ruff's eyes locked with those of Buffalo Killer. And for the very first time ever, Ruff knew what it was like to have someone hold his life in the palm of his hand, to give . . . or to take.

TWELVE

For reasons that Ruff would never figure if he lived to be one hundred, Monica Tucker, sensing that their fates were about to be sealed, began to sing a popular gospel. Perhaps it was her form of a prayer, maybe the child, sensing approaching death, felt inspired. More likely, she had been taught to sing and pray since earliest childhood and it came to her naturally. But whatever the reason, Monica sang.

"Amazing grace, how sweet the sound that saved a wretch like me I once was lost but now am found was blind but now I see."

The Comanche looked appalled. They tried to stare the child into a submissive silence. Even Ruff's first impulse was to clamp his hand over Moncia's mouth, but something told him to let her keep singing and the Comanche be damned.

"T'was grace that taught my heart to fear and grace my fears relieved How precious did that grace appear the hour I first believed."

When Monica's sweet voice faded, the Comanche had quieted. Looking into their eyes, Ruff was amazed to see that they had been touched by the child's song and perhaps even remembered when they were children and had sung to calm their own fears.

"This song the child sings, I like it," Buffalo Killer finally said. "Why does she sing now?"

"I don't know," Ruff replied, looking down at the girl. "Monica, why did you just begin to sing?"

Monica looked at the Comanche chief and then at the other warriors. "I thought that bad things were going to happen to my mommy and daddy. Mommy told me that whenever I got too scared to pray, I could sing gospels instead. So I did."

Buffalo Killer jammed his rifle into the scabbard tied to his saddle. "These are Cherokee people?"

"Part Cherokee. This child's father is a preacher. A man of God. He is kind and honest. At the same time, he is brave and will fight to protect his family. This I have seen on the banks of the Trinity River, where we had to kill bone pickers, and then we took their mules and wagons."

"He is foolish to cross Comanche land," Buffalo Killer replied. He looked to his warriors and made a decision. "Tell this man to come out of the trees. Tell them all to come out of the trees."

"And you will not allow your warriors to harm them?"

Buffalo Killer spoke, not to Ruff, but to his men. "We talk to these Cherokee people. Maybe they give us some presents for crossing our land."

The Comanche gave no indication they heard or understood, but Ruff knew that they had done both. He wanted to squeeze Monica because of his joy and relief, but instead he calmly replied, "Thank you, Buffalo Killer."

"Go tell them we come in peace asking only payment for crossing our land."

The two warriors that Ruff had beaten the day before

were furious and began to argue as Ruff urged High Fire into a lope. Ruff did not look back but he was damned sure that at least three of the Comanche would have put bullets through his back had it not been for Buffalo Killer's iron will.

When he entered the grove of trees, Dixie, Anna, and the Tucker children ran forward, hugging Ruff and Monica while deluging him with questions about the Comanche.

"Wait a minute!" Ruff finally ordered, stepping back into this saddle. "Let me talk."

"Are they going to kill us?" Anna asked. "Yes or no!"

Ruff shook his head. "All I can say for certain is that I don't think I would have gotten her to Austin alive. Even if I had, I doubt any doctor could have saved her. But the Comanche medicine man used poultices and prayer to draw out the snake venom."

"Would he do the same for my husband?" Anna blurted. "His leg is infected from the knee down. It doesn't look good, Ruff, so if there is a Comanche cure, we'd better try it now."

"We can ask Calling Hawk to use his medicine again," Ruff said.

"What will they do to us?"

"I think they'll want horses, rifles, and such but then they'll leave us alone. It's all up to their leader, Buffalo Killer."

Dixie turned and peered through the trees. "Which one is he?"

"The man on the pinto stud."

Dixie studied the chief for a moment, then looked back at Ruff. "You haven't told me what happened to High Fire yet. He looks like he's been mauled by a bear."

"I'll tell you later," Ruff said. "But right now, we'd better not keep those Comanche waiting."

Anna looked up from hugging Monica. "Are you sure they won't kill us?"

Ruff thought about that for a moment before he said, "My gut tells me we'll be all right unless one of the warriors loses control. Buffalo Killer is a strong leader. I think he respects me and Monica and I don't believe he is bloodthirsty, Mrs. Tucker."

"All right. I never thought I'd see Monica alive again and now I'll accept your judgment on this matter. If you're wrong, I pray that my children will be spared."

"Then we'd better get moving," Ruff said.

Dixie began to get the children ready to meet the Comanche hunting party, instructing each that they should act brave and try to smile. Most of all, they should not stare at the fierce-looking Comanche, for that would make them angry.

"All right," she said, "we're ready."

Ruff tied High Fire to a tree. "Has anyone explained this to your husband yet?"

"He's delirious," Dixie said.

Ruff heard the ominous tone of her voice and it made him realize that the reverend was in bad shape. Either the snakebite had become infected or else it had poisoned the bottom half of his leg. Even without seeing the man, Ruff knew that Moody Tucker was most likely dying.

But how could that be when his small child had survived? Ruff had no clear answer to that puzzling question. All he could do was remember how a grown man had once been stung by a bumblebee and had swollen up like a watermelon, then died. As boys, Ruff and his brothers had been stung many, many times without suffering any real consequences. Ruff supposed it was the same with snake-bites—some people could shrug them off, others suffered a fatal reaction.

"Let's go," he said, gathering the children together.

"What do we do when we meet them?" Dixie blurted.

Ruff thought a moment, then he took Moncia's hand and said, "Will you lead us in the last stanza of 'Amazing Grace'?" Buffalo Killer had liked that gospel and it even seemed to have a peaceful effect on his warriors.

She dipped her chin and even managed a smile, which was noted by all the other Tucker children. "They're not so mean and awful," she said to her frightened brothers and sisters. "Some of them are even pretty nice."

That broke the ice and lifted everyone's spirits. And before they lost their nerve, Ruff led Monica and the rest of the family out of the trees and straight for the Comanche hunting party. He just hoped and prayed that Long Bow or one of the other two men who'd suffered at his hands did not lose control and open fire on the women and the children.

When they were within fifty yards of the unsmiling Comanche, the Tucker family began to sing. Their voices lifted and soared as if they were an entire church choir and they probably had been at their revival tent back in Saugus, Oklahoma. They sounded very, very good, and when Ruff glanced sideways at Dixie, he could see that her eyes were shining with the same kind of pride he was feeling inside.

"When we've been here ten thousand years bright shining as the sun. We've no less days to sing God's praise then when we first begun."

Buffalo Killer raised his hand in greeting and studied the family for a moment. He studied Dixie, who had long dark hair and Ruff's prominent cheekbones. "Cherokee?"

"My mother was a half-breed," Dixie answered. "She died taking care of her people in the Great Smoky Mountains of Tennessee."

Next, he looked to Anna Tucker. With her pale skin and blue eyes, she didn't look as if she had a drop of American Indian blood in her veins. "Cherokee?"

Ruff's heart skipped a beat when the woman said, "No. But my husband is a quarter Cherokee and that makes each of our children an eighth Cherokee."

Anna gathered her frightened children around her like a hen her chicks. "All of them have Cherokee Indian blood in their veins."

"Where is your man?"

"He was bitten by snakes, just like my daughter, whose life you saved. He needs our prayers."

"Calling Hawk has strong medicine," Buffalo Killer told her.

Anna Tucker looked past the chief. "Which one of you is Calling Hawk?"

Ruff turned his gaze to the medicine man and then everyone looked at him. Calling Hawk raised his chin. He did not speak but a few words of English but certainly recognized his name.

Anna left her children and hurried forward. When she came to the medicine man's side, she looked up at him and said, "I owe you more than my life, Calling Hawk."

The medicine man looked uncomfortable. Even more so when Anna removed her gold wedding band and held it up to Calling Hawk.

"Take it, please. Take it and use your powers to also save my husband's life. If you do that, you can have everything we own. Everything, Calling Hawk."

Most of the Comanche understood and those that did not could not have failed to detect the desperation and urgency in Anna's pleading voice. Ruff stepped forward and gently placed his hands on the woman's shoulders. He drew her away from the embarrassed medicine man saying, "Calling

Hawk will consider your appeal, Mrs. Tucker. Maybe later, he would accept your ring or some other token of your appreciation."

"Please help him!" Anna cried as Ruff pulled her back from the knot of mounted Comanche.

Dixie came to the distraught woman's side. She looked up at Buffalo Killer. "Show me your Comanche medicine."

Calling Hawk looked away but some of the Comanche who understood laughed. Buffalo Killer was amused. "Ruff," he said, "this sister of yours is very brave. I like her."

"So do I," Ruff said, hoping that Buffalo Killer did not like Dixie too much. "She's just a girl of fifteen summers."

But Buffalo Killer saw Dixie in a different light. "Fine woman," he said.

And then he motioned for Ruff to lead his Comanche warriors into the trees, where they would make camp and decide what to do with the whites.

THIRTEEN

The Tucker children, not having seen the massacred couple up near the Trinity River, were quickly at ease with the Comanche. Soon they were showing the warriors simple prizes, a pretty rock, a piece of wood that was shaped like a turtle, a few shiny buttons. They had lost all their real toys in the Red River and so their treasures were as simple as those of Indian children. This impressed the Comanche.

The youngest of them, a genial-appearing warrior named Little Wolf, took obvious delight in the children. He carved them little figures with amazing speed. He could turn out a wooden horse or a dog—which looked almost the same, except the horse had a mane and thicker tail—in minutes. And although he tried to look somber and reserved as befitting a member of Buffalo Killer's hunting party, he was soon dashing around in the cottonwood grove, laughing and playing with the Tucker children.

This caused some of the older warriors to grumble and scowl. But a few clearly approved and even foraged through the heavy woods to make sure that there were no more rattlesnakes.

After some serious coaxing, Calling Hawk allowed himself to be talked into examining Reverend Tucker. The moment Ruff saw the Tucker's gangrenous leg, he was shocked, and it must have shown on his face because Anna burst into tears.

"He's dying, isn't he!" she choked.

Ruff laid his hand on the reverend's forehead. Like his daughter a few days earlier, Tucker was raging with a fever.

"I don't think anyone can save that leg," Dixie whispered in Ruff's ear.

Calling Hawk had no doubt seen gangrene before. After all, his tribesmen were hunters and fighters. In their rough, outdoor world, it was expected that bones would sometimes be broken and warriors would suffer often fatal injuries. Calling Hawk accepted Reverend Tucker's snakebite as a fatal injury. Without emotion or preamble, he began a death chant.

Ruff was inclined to agree with the Comanche medicine man's evaluation. It shocked him when he recalled how robust and vital this man of God had been been when they'd first met in Saugus, Oklahoma. It did not help to also remember how much the reverend had been respected among the Cherokee. They'd given him and his family a hundred dollars, and Tucker had given it back to a poor, grieving old lady. Ruff knew that if he died Reverend Moody Tucker would be sorely missed on the frontier. The man was probably not over fifty years old and he still had a lot of sinners to save.

"Ruff?"

He looked at Dixie, who motioned him aside. She leaned close so that she could not be overheard. "The leg has to come off if there's any chance of him surviving. Don't you agree?"

"I don't know," Ruff said, "maybe Calling Hawk can do something with his poultices."

"That's ridiculous and you know it," Dixie said. "The

leg is rotting from the knee down. It will have to come off if the reverend has any hope of surviving the next few days."

Ruff felt sweat began to trickle down his spine. "What are you suggesting, that we cut if off?"

"Yes."

"That's crazy!"

Dixie grabbed his arm and led him a little deeper into the woods. "Listen," Dixie said, "do you remember Mason telling us about how he'd assisted the Confederate army doctors in sawing off legs and arms? He explained exactly how they operated and it didn't seem that difficult. I recall Mason saying that, after a battle, those frenzied army doctors would remove hundreds of limbs in a single day, never spending more than ten or fifteen minutes with each."

"But they were doctors! And they must have had medicines or . . . or at least whiskey."

"We have whiskey," Dixie said excitedly. "The children found several bottles in those piles of bones. I found even more in a special little box stashed under one of the wagons. Those men hid their bottles from each other. Altogether, we've probably got a gallon of the stuff."

"The reverend would never—"

"He's *delirious,* Ruff! We can pour it down his throat, a whole bottleful."

"That might kill him."

"He's going to die for sure if we don't liquor him up and cut off that leg."

Ruff shook his head because he wanted no part of cutting off anyone's leg. What he wanted was for Calling Hawk to pull another miracle out of his medicine bag and save Tucker. But deep inside, Ruff knew that it was not going to happen. No poultice in the world, no matter how powerful its medicinal effect, could draw the poison from such a terrible leg infection.

"Ruff, it's his only chance!" Dixie whispered. "Maybe Calling Hawk can help us stop the bleeding or prevent any more gangrene by applying his Indian medicine. Maybe not. Either way, we need to do this right now."

"But we don't have a surgical saw to cut through the heavy leg bones."

"We won't have to," she told him. "We can do the amputation at the knee joint."

Ruff realized she was right. The knee joint was a natural place to amputate. But getting the leg off was only half the problem. "He'll bleed to death if we don't cauterize the stump the instant the leg is severed."

"I know." Dixie touched her brother's arm. "I remember Mason saying that the doctors splashed whiskey over the leg both just before and just after an amputation."

"Why?"

Dixie shrugged her shoulders. "They just seemed to think that it made the amputated limb heal better."

Ruff took a deep breath. Everything inside of him revolted at the thought of amputating the reverend's leg from the knee down. He was sure that the man would either die of shock or blood loss.

"What about Calling Hawk?" Dixie asked. "He's probably not going to be too happy when he learns of our plans. As it stands right now, he's the center of attention and I have the impression he'd have it no other way."

"I'll see what I can do about him," Ruff replied. "Get the whiskey and have Mrs. Tucker get a fire burning. Find something metal that I can use to do the cauterizing. It has to be big, Dixie."

Dixie started to leave but Ruff caught her by the arm. "Will Anna allow this operation?"

"If you hadn't arrived, we were going to try and do it ourselves today," Dixie said. "We've talked of nothing else for days. She knows that the gangrene is poisoning his whole body and it has to be removed and very soon."

"Maybe she'll take heart now that Calling Hawk is here. After all, he did save Monica."

"Yes," Dixie agreed, "he did. But Monica had a fever, not gangrene."

Ruff knew the point was well taken. "All right," he said, "just make sure we have red-hot metal when that leg comes off. Otherwise, the reverend will bleed to death in minutes. I'd also like to keep Anna away from us."

"I'll ask her to stay by the fire and have an extra cauterizing implement ready, just in case."

"And you'll handle Calling Hawk and Buffalo Killer?"

"I'll do what I can," he said. "I don't see why they'll object. After all, it's not their leg we're going to hack off at the knee."

As Dixie hurried off to find Anna Tucker, she snapped, "Rufus Ballou, you certainly don't respect the delicacies of speech."

Ruff didn't have time to consider his alleged transgression. He was tired and dreading like hell the next hour and the prospect of removing half a leg. He drew his bowie knife from its sheath and tested its edge on his thumbnail. The bowie had been forged in New Orleans and was of the finest steel. Justin Ballou had specially ordered each of his sons the same extraordinary knife on their sixteenth birthday. Ruff's three older brothers who'd died in the war had lost theirs on the battlefield. Houston had lost his as well, most likely stolen in a Mississippi brothel. Ruff's knife was the only one left, and he was extremely proud of the weapon. Even so, it wasn't a scalpel and he damn sure wasn't a surgeon.

• • •

"Is everything ready?"

Dixie nodded. They had poured the best part of a bottle down Reverend Tucker's throat. If he survived this operation, Ruff knew the man was going to have a monumental hangover. It would be a blessing, since Ruff didn't think the reverend had much of a chance of coming out of this operation alive.

Dixie glanced at Calling Hawk, who had the job of dousing the leg just before and after the amputation. "Is *he* ready?"

Calling Hawk had not taken the news of their decision to remove the leg with as much grace as Ruff would have hoped. The Comanche medicine man had suddenly gone from being the focal point of this life-or-death drama to being a mere bystander, a douser of whiskey. As such, he was very unhappy and had drowned his disappointment in whiskey.

Standing nearby with his second bottle, Calling Hawk was already swaying back and forth, eyes glassy and unfocused. Ruff had never seen anyone drink so hard or fast.

"He's going to pass out before this is over," Ruff predicted.

He motioned for Calling Hawk to give him the bottle so that he could pour the rest of it down the reverend's throat. Not unpredictably, the Comanche medicine man shook his head in refusal.

"The hell with him," Ruff snapped. "Dixie, give me another bottle."

Dixie handed him a bottle, which Ruff uncorked. Staring at the black, stinking leg, he felt his stomach lurch with nausea. To quell it, Ruff upended the bottle and took a several huge gulps. Choking, he wiped tears from his eyes and drew a deep breath.

"Are you ready now?" Dixie asked, her voice openly disapproving.

"Yeah," Ruff said. "Let's get his over with."

He turned and looked at Calling Hawk. "Do it," he ordered, motioning the medicine man to splash some whiskey on the knee.

Calling Hawk's lip twisted in a defiant sneer. He proclaimed his independence by taking another long pull on the bottle, sucking it empty.

"Forget him," Ruff said, turning his back on the medicine man and dousing the knee with his own bottle. "Let's go."

Dixie had gathered a pile of linen. Clean shirts, dresses, anything they could find to use as bandaging. Ruff studied the knee, which was the uppermost limit of the infection. It was darker than normal and swollen. It felt hot but it was not yet infected.

"I don't quite know how to start," he confessed as doubts flooded over him like great ocean waves.

"Just cut it off," Dixie said, a tremor in her own voice. "After that we'll do whatever we can."

Ruff took a deep breath and massaged the kneecap. "I'm going to try and go under it," he said. "As soon as I can, I'll find the joint and that's where I'll sever the leg."

"Stop talking and start cutting," Dixie whispered.

Ruff said a little prayer and then he placed the blade of his sharp bowie knife just below the knee and pressed down hard as he made a deep incision through flesh. Blood poured out of the wound across his hand. Reverend Tucker's body convulsed and a groan escaped from his mouth. But mercifully, he slipped deeper into unconsciousness.

Ruff knew there was no stopping now. The reverend was bleeding heavily and he had to get the leg off in a hurry, then attempt to stop the bleeding. He felt his bowie strike bone, and he twisted the blade a little and used the heavy steel almost like a saw as he cut through tendon, cartilage, and muscle.

Sweat globules burst across Ruff's forehead like raindrops striking a flat rock. He closed his eyes and just kept sawing and grinding with the heavy bowie knife. He was feeling for the joint and when he found it, he sliced on through until his blade struck the blanket and then cut into the earth below.

Ruff opened his eyes and he saw Buffalo Killer hovering above him. The chief grabbed the severed leg and hurled it aside. Veins and arteries spurted blood and Ruff shouted for the cauterizing iron.

It was a flat piece of steel from a shovel head and it almost glowed with heat as Ruff slapped it against the hemorrhaging stump.

"Aggggh!" Tucker screamed, his entire body coming off the ground. Roused from his semiconscious state, the powerful man began to buck and thrash. Smoke and the stench of burning hair and flesh tormented Ruff's sensibilities. He fought off a wave of nausea and dizziness.

"Hold him!" Ruff shouted, bearing down even harder with the burning metal shovel head.

Buffalo Killer fell on the reverend and even Calling Hawk responded, throwing his weight on the man. Ruff's arm muscles corded as he struggled to hold the shovel head against the stump. He could hear the blood sizzle and over that, he could hear the reverend making terrible gurgling sounds as his body heaved and whipped back and forth in mindless agony.

Without the Comanche, they'd never have been able to keep the reverend pinned to the earth while Ruff cauterized the vessels until they were a charred, seeping mass.

"Bandages," he choked.

The bandages were brought to Ruff and he pressed them to

the stump and held them until the reverend's body slumped and went limp.

Dixie scooted around to his side. "Are you all right?"

"Yes. But we'd have lost it without Buffalo Killer and Calling Hawk."

The two Comanche climbed to their feet. Calling Hawk reached for the whiskey bottle at Ruff's side but his chief knocked it aside and pushed the drunken medicine man away. Calling Hawk stumbled into the woods.

"Maybe Tucker live anyway," Buffalo Killer said, looking first at Ruff, then deeply into Dixie's eyes. "Maybe we make strong white man's medicine."

"Tell Calling Hawk that we're going to need all his powers in the days ahead if this man is to survive," Ruff said. "His work is just beginning—if he wants to help."

"He help."

Buffalo Killer looked closely at Dixie. "You have a man?"

She was spattered with blood, pale and shaken, but the Comanche chief's words snapped her head back with alarm. "Yes," she blurted. "I have a man."

"Who?"

Dixie threw her eyes to Ruff, silently pleading for help. Ruff did not know what to say. He did not want to lie to this chief, but it was obvious that Buffalo Killer was showing a sexual interest in his kid sister.

"His name," Ruff said slowly, "is High Man."

"High Man?" The Comanche was very displeased.

"Yes," Dixie said. "High Man."

"Cherokee?"

"No . . . Thoroughbred."

Buffalo Killer's lip curled with contempt. "Never hear of that Indian people. Must be weak! Not like Comanche, who are strong."

Dixie lowered her eyes to the bandage, which had already become blood-soaked. She quickly replaced it and, to her credit, she said nothing more, and neither did Ruff until the chief and his medicine man left them with the reverend.

"Thoroughbred?" Ruff asked, expelling a deep breath he'd been holding.

Dixie shrugged. "It was the truth, wasn't it?"

"Yes," Ruff admitted, "but if he ever finds out that is our breed of horses, he'll kill the both of us."

"Oh well," Dixie said, dismissing the matter as she focused all of her attention on saving their patient.

FOURTEEN

Reverend Moody Tucker hovered between life and death for forty-eight hours before his fever broke and he opened his eyes. He looked up at his family crowded all around, blinked, and forced a thin smile.

"It looks like heaven, but forgive me, Lord, I feel like hell."

Anna Tucker sobbed and hugged her husband, and the children nearly suffocated their father. When he recognized Monica, the reverend broke down and wept tears of gratitude.

Ruff stepped forward to introduce the Comanche. "Reverend, this is Chief Buffalo Killer, who spared our lives, and his medicine man, Calling Hawk, who saved Monica."

Reverend Tucker's voice was just strong enough so that they all heard him say, "I'll pray for you always to my Lord and you are welcome to the few material goods my family possesses. Everything. All we ask is safe passage to Austin."

Buffalo Killer dipped his chin in assent, then he folded his hands behind his back and walked slowly into the trees to consider what he had seen among the whites. Maybe, Ruff wondered, the Comanche chief was seeing that white people could be as good and generous as his own Indian people and that their children could be as grateful.

It was another three days before they were confident that the reverend could physically stand the rigors of wagon travel. During that time, Buffalo Killer led his Comanche across the eastern Texas grasslands searching for the last scattered herds of buffalo or the fleet and wary antelope. Because he rode High Fire and quickly proved himself a marksman with his Spencer rifle, Ruff was allowed to join the hunting party.

Hunting with the Comanche was one of the most exciting experiences of Ruff's life. It was an almost indescribable thrill to gallop across the face of the earth, sandwiched between layers of waving grass and azure skies as they searched for game. When they flushed antelope, Ruff would allow High Fire to surge to the fore and they would race after the antelope, upright in their stirrups and firing their rifles. Sometimes, they would leap from their mounts, take a solid firing position, and put their shooting skills to the ultimate test as they attempted to drop the incredibly fast antelope.

The one time they found a small herd of buffalo, the Comanche went wild with happiness. They howled and charged into the herd, firing arrows and bullets. When they had killed four massive bulls, they allowed the others to escape to be hunted another day.

Normally squaws would have done the butchering, skinning, cooking, curing, and packing of meat, but these were not normal times, so the warriors had no choice but to scrape and stretch the hides and smoke the meat. And while doing this, they became like boys, laughing and teasing each other, calling one another girls and old women. With his hands and arms covered with blood and buffalo fat, Ruff felt one with these people, and they seemed to regard him as Comanche. When he declined to swallow a length of the slick, greasy intestine that the Comanche fed down their throats with relish, Ruff was teased unmercifully. That night, when they returned to the Tucker camp, everyone feasted in celebration, consuming enormous quantities of buffalo meat.

The next morning, Buffalo Killer and several of his men came to Ruff. "Comanche go now," the chief said. "Take tall, red horse, tall mares and one wagon."

Ruff's heart sank to learn that Buffalo Killer wanted High Fire and the last of their Tennessee Ballou mares which were his father's only legacy. Ruff understood that Buffalo Killer was within his rights to expect such prized gifts, but even so, Ruff could scarcely bear to think about losing his magnificent Thoroughbreds. The Comanche wanted every horse he and Dixie had brought from Tennessee except the old stallion High Man.

"Chief Buffalo Killer," Ruff said, chosing his words with great care. "These horses were my father's life. He is in their blood. My heart breaks to give so much of my father away, even to a great Comanche chief."

Buffalo Killer's face darkened and Ruff said quickly, "I offer a better trade. I offer you instead four rifles—all Spencer repeating rifles and four Colt revolvers."

The Comanche chief's eyes widened with surprise, for no horse was worth more than one of the new Spencer repeating rifles, which had been hidden from view under the bones.

"But," Ruff added quickly, "I want one other thing in trade. A small white boy whose parents were killed was taken by the Indians. I wish to return the boy to his own people."

"I do not know of this boy," Buffalo Killer said.

"I believe you, but I saw the Indian lances. In fact, I kept their feathers."

"Bring them to show Buffalo Killer."

Ruff hurried over to his saddlebags. He returned a few minutes later with the feathers he had taken from the lances. He also had one of the arrows he'd pulled from the dog that had been pincushioned.

"Kiowa," Buffalo Killer pronounced.

"Kiowa?" Ruff was caught off guard. "This far south?"

"Kiowa!"

"I would like to have this boy back," Ruff persisted stubbornly, knowing he would never have a second chance to broach this delicate subject. "If you help me get him back, I will give you the tall horse in return. You will have this horse and also the weapons."

"Ruff!"

Ruff ignored his sister. "I ask only to be allowed to take my people to Austin and then I will return and we will hunt for the boy."

"Maybe dead."

"Maybe."

"Maybe never find Kiowa."

"Maybe." Ruff squared his shoulders. "Kiowa are your traditional enemies, true?"

Buffalo Killer nodded impassively.

"Then I will help you hunt and kill them. In return, I want only the boy and one old pony to ride back to Austin."

Buffalo Killer stared into Ruff's eyes for a moment and then he turned and went to rejoin his warriors. Ruff knew that the chief would talk to them about this offer.

"Ruff, are you crazy!" Dixie whispred. "You'll get yourself killed and there's almost no chance of finding that band of murdering Kiowa."

"I have to try," Ruff said. "I've been thinking about it off and on for over a week. There is no way that I can rescue the boy by myself."

"But. . . ."

"They'll help me," Ruff said, feeling sure that Buffalo Killer would take his offer as a challenge. "The chief wants my horse. The only thing that he might want more than High Fire is *you,* Dixie."

"Rufus!"

"It's true," he said, managing a grin. "I think he'd agree to my terms in the snap of my fingers if I'd offered you instead of High Fire."

Dixie was incensed. "You ought to wash your mouth out with lye soap!"

Ruff chuckled in spite of the gravity of the circumstances and the tension he felt pulling at his gut like wet rawhide tightening in the sun. "Maybe so, but it *is* the truth."

"What makes you think he'd trust us after we reached the safety of Austin?"

"He knows me," Ruff said simply.

Dixie didn't argue the point. "If I lost you, I'd be the last Ballou."

"Houston said he'd return after the war."

"Damn Houston!" Dixie exploded. "He thinks of nothing but himself."

"That's not true," Ruff said, surprised and dismayed by her anger. "And you shouldn't say such things about your brother."

"It's because Houston *is* my brother that I can say such things," Dixie answered. "Houston never gave me a minute of his time all the while I was growing up at Wildwood Farm. But, Ruff, if I lost you . . ."

Ruff placed his forefinger over Dixie's lips. "Listen to me," he said. "I *have* to try and save that boy. I can't really explain to you why. I don't fully understand it myself. All I know is that it's something that I have to do."

"Even if you did find and rescue him," Dixie said, "do you realize what giving up High Fire means?"

"It means a great deal. But his father, High Man, is still a potent sire. Beside, I've been watching these Comanche and their horses. To be honest, maybe pure Thoroughbred is not the best-suited horse for this rough country."

"What is that supposed to mean?" Dixie demanded.

"When I had Monica and the Comanche were chasing me, I realized that their mustang ponies possess an incredible endurance. So I was thinking that if we could breed the best of their mustang mares to our stallions, we might have something very special. And ideally suited for the West."

"Ruff!" Dixie was appalled. "Our father spent the best years of his life breeding the finest Thoroughbreds in the South. And now you're talking about cross-breeding them with what—mustang scrubs!"

Ruff shook his head. "Dixie, you didn't see those Indians chasing me. Their ponies are not only fast and more agile than any Thoroughbred, but they are tireless. And they're perfectly adapted to the West. You see, because they're smaller they can survive and even stay fat on much less feed. Their hooves are like iron, so they don't crack or split, and that means they never need shoeing."

"I disagree," Dixie said, shaking her head adamantly. "Thoroughbreds are the the finest horses in the world."

"In Europe and in the East, yes. But not west of the Mississippi."

Ruff sighed. "This discussion is pointless for the time being. I've made an offer to Buffalo Killer to trade High Fire and our mares for a boy's freedom. It's a good trade and one that I will stand by. I'd just wish it's one you could accept."

Dixie's eyes filled with tears. She threw her arms around Ruff and hugged him with all her might. "Dammit, Rufus Ballou! You just be careful!"

"I will," he promised. "If that boy is alive, I'll find him and bring him back to you in Austin—God and Buffalo Killer willing."

Ruff held his sister until Buffalo Killer returned. The chief said, "We will ride together, Ruff. Find and kill Kiowa and maybe get boy. You give tall horse, four rifles, and guns."

"Yes. Win or lose."

"Good. Or I kill you," Buffalo Killer said matter-of-factly.

Ruff nodded. He'd anticipated that would also be part of this hard bargain.

Four days later, they saw Austin in the distance, a mushrooming colony of log cabins and clapboard houses that marked the capital of Texas. It was a sight that raised the reverend up on his bed of bones, offering thanks and prayer for delivering him to their new home.

When they were still about three miles north of capital, Buffalo Killer rode up to the bone wagon that Ruff was driving and stared at him.

"He's telling me it's time I join him," Ruff said, handing his reins to Dixie.

Ruff sensed that his kid sister was going to do something foolish, like trying to talk him into welching on his bargain. He cut off her protest by saying, "The Comanche have come to respect me, Dixie. I may die out there, but it won't be at their hands. So you just stay in Austin and help the Tuckers get settled. Take good care of High Man and our mares."

Dixie nodded and Ruff could see that she was struggling to make a brave show of his leaving. He said, "I'll be all right. And I'll come back."

"Sure." Dixie tried to smile and it broke Ruff's heart to watch. Even Buffalo Killer, understanding the love between a brother and his only sister, felt the need to look away.

Ruff jumped down from the seat of the bone wagon. "Dixie, before Houston left us in the Indian Territory to go to Washington to find Molly O'Day, I told him to keep in touch by sending letters care of the governor of Texas."

"The governor?"

Ruff shrugged. "I didn't know where else he should send them in care of. I knew that even in wartime, Texas would still have a governor. Find out who he is and if he received a letter from Houston."

"I will," Dixie promised.

Ruff knew that there were a lot of other things that he should say, but he couldn't get the words out so he just turned around and went back to saddle High Fire and say good-bye to the Tucker family. He'd always hated good-byes and this one didn't do a damn thing to change that feeling.

Fifteen minutes later he was in the saddle and galloping north with the Comanche. It was well over a hundred miles back to the burned-out emigrant wagon and the starting point of the murdering Kiowa's trail. A trail, Ruff knew, that might lead them all to an early grave.

FIFTEEN

Dixie Ballou liked everything about Austin, Texas. It was an interesting and scenic town perfectly suited to the temperment of its frontier people. Situated on a sweeping bend of the Colorado River, it was far less humid than the former capital of Houston. The air was brisk and it generally cooled off, even on the hottest days of summer and early autumn. The original name of the settlement had been Waterloo, but that had been more than thirty years earlier, before the site was named after the father of Texas, Stephen Austin.

Back in the autumn of 1839, Republic of Texas president Mirabeau Lamar had instructed five horsemen to pick the most ideal location possible for his new capital, and Austin had been their unqualified first choice. Later, General Sam Houston had moved the capital to Houston but that had not lasted, and in 1850, against Houston's iron will, the Texas legislature had voted to make Austin their permanent capital. This despite it being on the very edge of Texas's wild northern frontier dominated by the bold Comanche.

Unlike most western settlements that grew haphazardly around a fort or trading post, Austin been laid out by a qualified surveyor so that city's roads were a neat, easily expandable grid centered by Congress Avenue. As a precaution against Comanche raiders, an eight-foot-high stockade had initially been erected around the capitol building itself. Despite this precaution, during the first few years, the Comanche often did sneak into the settlement to rob and even scalp the unwary citizens of Austin.

By the 1850s, the Comanche threat was waning. Elegant public buildings had begun to replace Austin's earlier collection of log cabins and the town had an air of solid permanence. A fine new capitol building was erected, along with a governor's mansion, a land office, schools, a hospital with balconies and a dome, meeting halls, prospering businesses, and churches. From that point onward, Austin had an air of respectability not often found on the wild Texas frontier.

On the afternoon that Dixie and the Tucker family arrived in Austin, a horse race was in progress, and although Dixie would have loved to stop and watch the race, which had attracted a big crowd, she knew that it was not possible. The reverend was still unwell and in immediate need of a doctor's care to ensure that the amputation did not become infected. Also, Mrs. Tucker and her children were thin and very tired.

But even so, as they drove down broad Congress Avenue, Reverend Tucker could be heard calling out from his perch high on top of the bone wagon, "Good afternoon, my brothers and sisters! I am the Reverend Moody T. Tucker, humble servant of the Lord and minister of the Gospel Fire Church! Brethren, we'll be having an old-fashioned revival in just a few days! We'll sing and praise the Lord!"

"Hey," a saloon keeper yelled with a broad grin, "are you really going to preach from the top of that there pile of bones!"

"Ashes to ashes, dust to dust," Tucker shouted, "it does make a suitable pulpit to remind us of our universal mortality."

The saloon keeper nodded. "Good point, preacher! You'll

find a few willing hearts and open minds! But don't you go preachin' on the evils of drink, now! I've got this world's business to attend to before leaving for the next."

"Can you tell me which of these fine establishments is owned by my brother-in-law, Mr. Roscoe Cudworth?"

"You're Cudworth's brother-in-law!"

"That I am!"

"Hee-haw!" the saloon keeper howled. "And did you come to settle in with him?"

"The Lord expects us all to share his blessings."

"Hee-haw!" the man howled even louder. "You just keep them stinkin' bone wagons movin' for another block and pull 'em right up in front of Cudworth's Mercantile. Can't miss it on the right! And tell that old skinflint that Homer Banes sends his condolences!"

Dixie was driving the lead wagon and followed the directions. She could still hear the saloon keeper's braying laughter and wondered what Banes had thought so funny.

The Cudworth Mercantile was impressive. In fact, it appeared to Dixie a little run down compared to its neighboring businesses. But when the reverend and his wife saw it, they made such a fuss you'd have thought that Cudworth's Mercantile was the biggest thing west of the Mississippi River.

Dixie jumped down from her seat and the Tucker children swarmed off the second bone wagon like attacking hornets. Tucker himself got so excited that he didn't wait for help and tumbled off the bone pile and landed smack in the street, stump waving.

Dixie was appalled. If the reverend had landed on the stump, it would certainly have ruptured the blood vessels and caused massive bleeding. Mrs. Tucker was shouting and yelling for her children to settle down and a curious crowd was gathering to watch. And then the saloon keeper came running up and shouting to everyone on the street, "There's Cudworth's family come to Texas! That preacher is Mrs. Cudworth's brother!"

This bit of news caused a great stir and no small amount of guffaws and tittering among the women. "Maybe Cudworth will give you a few cents off on a pair of crutches, preacher!" someone yelled.

Dixie marched right up and slapped the cruel jester.

"Shame on you! The Reverend Tucker and his family have suffered terribly on the way down from Oklahoma. Before they left, they had a wagon but they lost it in the Red River. And they gave all their money to a widow woman in Saugus even though it was all they had!"

Tucker balanced on one leg. His face was gray with pain and he had lost so much weight that folds of skin hung around his once thick neck like fleshy necklaces.

"Now, Miss Ballou," he said. "I'm sure that everyone in Texas has suffered their share of hardships but the Lord provides! And he'll provide us all with his love and bounty if we do not lose faith."

The townspeople weren't smirking anymore. The man that Dixie had slapped became so ashamed that he yanked out his wallet and dropped a dollar into his own hat. "We're glad to have you and your family, Reverend. And I think you're going to need more than your brother-in-law's help to feed your brood."

"Amen!" someone called as the hat was passed around.

In no time at all, the hat was overflowing and Mrs. Tucker was so overcome with gratitude that she had to blow her nose. Her husband thanked the crowd and again promised them an old-fashioned revival once he and his family had gotten settled in with the Cudworths.

After the crowd drifted away, the reverend stuffed the money into his pants pocket and said, "Yes sir, there are

good Christian hearts in Austin! We're all going to do just
fine here."

The front door of the store opened a crack, then it
slammed shut. A moment later, to everyone's amazement,
the shutters were drawn and a Closed sign was slipped into
the window.

"Huh," the reverend said, extracting his pocket watch. "I
don't think my watch stopped and it says that it's only four
o'clock. Not time for a normal workday closing."

Dixie did not know what to say but her sense of fore-
boding was growing by the second.

"Help me up to the door," the reverend said to his wife.
"Children, you're about to meet your Uncle Roscoe, so be
on your best behavior."

"We're all so dirty," Anna fretted. "And none of us smell
very good, either. I do hope that we don't make a terrible
first impression on your sister's husband."

"Ah," the reverend said, dismissing that possibility, "I've
never met the man, either, but I'm sure he'll understand the
circumstances and be overjoyed that we arrived alive and
in good health."

"I hope so," Anna said as she helped her husband up
onto the boardwalk and he hopped over to knock on the
mercantile's front door.

There was no answer. The reverend, balancing precari-
ously, knocked again and again. No answer.

A spectator shook his head and turned to leave. Dixie
hurried over to the man, leaned close so that she would not
be overheard, and whispered, "Do you know where we can
find Mr. Cudworth?"

"My guess is that Roscoe saw you through the window
and is hiding in the back room," the man said in an under-
tone. "He ain't the kind to welcome poor folks, family or
otherwise."

"Are you sure?"

"Yep. He has a reputation for being a miser and that's why some of the folks were getting such a laugh until you slapped Bert's face and made him realize what a fool he was making out of himself."

The man shifted his feet uncomfortably. "You'd better warn that poor family that Roscoe Cudworth is a hard, tight-fisted man that wouldn't give a crumb to a starving child if he thought he could save a hundred of 'em to squeeze together and make a slice of bread."

"Damn," Dixie muttered. "I was hoping that Cudworth was a good man."

"He's a tightwad," the stranger said. "Why, he owns half this city block but you'd never find him helping anyone out. He owns a bank and is his own richest customer. The first dollar Cudworth ever made is probably still locked up in his bank vault."

Dixie's heart sank. "Where do he and his wife live?"

"Go two blocks up the street, turn right on Second Street, and then left on Brazos. It'll be about a block down on the left. Big two-story redbrick mansion. Most people think it's probably the governor's mansion, but it ain't. It's just all for the two of them. Roscoe won't give a dime for any civic causes, but he sure doesn't mind spending money on himself."

"And they have no children?"

"No, thank the Lord. Roscoe would charge his children room and board and treat 'em worse than slaves."

"What about his wife?"

"She does whatever her husband wants. She's not allowed to spend any of Roscoe's money so she's become a hermit. Seems nice enough, but she's not seen about very much anymore."

Dixie trudged back to the Tucker family and gave them

the directions to the Cudworth house on Brazos Street. "Let's all load up and I'll lead the way."

"Come on, children," Reverend Tucker called, looking pale and shaky. "Let's go meet your aunt and uncle!"

They all loaded up again and Dixie drove the lead bone wagon on down to Second Street, turned right, and found Brazos. In less than five minutes, they were parked before a beautiful brick mansion.

"Here we are!" Dixie called, and she jumped off her wagon and went back to help the reverend down.

This time when they knocked on the door, it was opened by a tall, dignified-looking woman in a plain, shapeless dress. She had reddish hair pulled back into a tight bun and very pale blue eyes. Eyes that blinked in amazement and stared at Reverend Tucker, then dropped to the stump of his leg. Eyes that widened with sudden recognition.

"Moody?"

"Margaret!"

"Moody!"

Whereupon the reverend lurched forward and tried to hug his sister but missed and tumbled over the doorstep to crash against the marble floor.

"Moody!" she cried, dropping beside her brother. "Good heavens, what happened to you!"

As Dixie had feared, in his haste in getting on and off the bone wagon and because of this fall, the reverend's stump began to bleed.

"His leg has been amputated less than a week," Dixie explained when Mrs. Cudworth's eyes fluttered with shock and she threw her pale hands to her breast. "Your brother is not at all well."

"Dear heavens!" she cried, her eyes scattering across the rest of the family. "What on earth has happened to them!"

The reverend pushed himself into a sitting position and

grabbed his thigh, grimacing with pain. "The Lord always provides, Margaret, but for right now, you and Roscoe will have to take his place."

Dixie looked into Margaret's eyes and saw fear and uncertainty. Dixie said, "He needs you, Mrs. Cudworth. This whole family needs you like never before."

To the woman's credit and to Dixie's great relief, Margaret Cudworth squared her thin shoulders and said, "You and the children come on inside and we'll give you bedrooms and . . . and baths. And food, lots of food."

Dixie heard Anna stifle a little sigh of relief. Until hearing that, Dixie had not realized how worried Anna had been about this reception. The children flooded into the mansion. Raced across its marble floors and up its winding staircase.

"Children! Children!" the reverend croaked. "Behave yourselves!"

But the children didn't listen. They had never been in such a house before and might never be again.

"Let them enjoy themselves," Margaret said, helping Dixie and Anna drag the reverend to his foot. "Now let's get him upstairs to your bedroom and then I'll send for a doctor at once!"

"Not necessary," Moody breathed.

"The hell it isn't," Anna said, shocking both herself and her husband.

They managed to get the reverend upstairs but by then the bandages of his stump were a sodden with fresh blood. Dixie was scared they might even lose the reverend and that would be a terrible injustice considering all that the man had been through.

Less than ten minutes after their arrival, a handsome young doctor raced through the front door and flew up the stairs. He took one look at the bleeding stump upon which

Dixie was using a compress and said, "I'm going to have to tie off the bleeders. Can someone help me?"

"I will," Dixie said. "I helped my brother do the amputation."

"You and your brother did this?"

"Yes. He had gangrene. We had no choice and the Comanche helped."

"What a story this will be," the doctor said, opening his medical kit. "But let's concentrate on getting the bleeding stopped so that the story will have a happy ending."

"You bet," Dixie said. "Just tell me what to do and it's as good as done."

"I believe that," the doctor said. "I need hot water and plenty of bandages."

"I'll get them," Margaret Cudworth said, jumping up and racing off.

Anna looked ready to faint. Dixie said, "Why don't you take care of the children? If we need your help, we'll call."

"Promise?"

"Yes."

Anna nodded and hurried out of the room. Dixie could hear the woman praying all the way down the stairs.

"I'm going to live," Tucker said in a voice that was shockingly weak. "I can't die after all we've been through, the Lord willing."

The doctor nodded as he threaded a needle and said, "Forceps, please."

Dixie gave him the forceps but despite her best attempt to concentrate on helping the doctor, she was remembering Ruff's huge bowie knife and how it had cut off the lower half of the reverend's poor leg.

SIXTEEN

The doctor led Dixie out of the bedroom and closed the door, leaving his patient to sleep. "I gave him enough laudanum to put him out for twenty-four hours. I'll be back to check that amputation in a few hours."

"Thank you very much," Dixie said. "Between Mrs. Cudworth, Mrs. Tucker, and myself, we'll keep a constant watch over the reverend."

The doctor took Dixie's arm and led her a little farther down the second-story landing. "I don't want to sound unkind," he said, "but you and Mrs. Tucker look exhausted. Dead on your feet. I think that Mrs. Cudworth should watch over our patient while you and the poor man's wife sleep."

"Thanks," Dixie said, "but we'll be fine. Is there any danger of additional bleeding?"

"Not unless he bumps the injury, and that won't happen as long as he remains in bed."

Dixie nodded. Her eyes burned and she suddenly felt very, very weak, almost to the point of being dizzy. Maybe it was the mental stress in addition to the physical toll that had her reeling.

"Miss Ballou!"

Dixie realized that the doctor was supporting her. "I'm all right."

"You're not all right," the doctor argued. "I'm going to see that you go to bed right now. How old are you, young lady?"

"Fifteen. How old are you?" she challenged.

"Ten years your senior," he said, helping Dixie to her assigned bedroom. "And I've seen enough to know that you are out on your feet."

"I'll be fine," Dixie told him, sitting on the bed.

The doctor wrinkled his nose. "You people need baths and new clothes."

"It's those damned stinking buffalo bones," Dixie replied. "I stayed away from them but their smell gets into your hair and skin."

The doctor nodded. "Have you met Mr. Cudworth yet?"

"No, and from what I've heard so far, it's not going to be a pleasure." Dixie studied the doctor. He was of average height, with sandy brown hair, hazel eyes, and a whiskerless chin. Dr. William Gentry didn't look much older than herself and certainly much too young to be a college educated doctor.

"Mr. Cudworth is a very . . . difficult man," the doctor told her. "Quite frankly, he's a miser. I can't recall him doing a single good deed for the people of Austin, but he is a gifted businessman. I've heard it jokingly said that if he bought his own cemetery plot, it would turn out to be a verticle shaft of pure gold. He's that lucky with his investments."

"Do you think he will throw us out?"

The doctor shrugged. "The thought has entered my mind."

"The reverend is dead broke. We can probably sell the bone wagons and the two teams of mules, but that would be all he and his family have in this world."

"There's no market for bones here in Austin. In Houston,

they cart them down to the harbor and put them on ships bound for the East Coast. But up here . . . well, you won't get much of anything for them."

"The wagons will be worth something and so will the mules," Dixie said. "I'll find a buyer."

"I'll help you," the doctor promised. "And there's something else that has entered my mind."

"What?"

Before the doctor could explain, the front door slammed and they heard a shout, "Margaret!"

"He's here," Dr. Gentry said. "Brace yourself for all hell let loose."

"What . . ."

"*Margaret! What are these filthy children doing in our house!*"

Margaret Cudworth rushed out of the reverend's bedroom and grabbed the downstairs railing. She looked down at her husband, a tall, reed-thin man, bald on top, with tufts of black hair exploding out from his temples.

"Mr. Cudworth, those children are your nephews! My brother Moody and his family have arrived."

Cudworth looked up and his face was blistered with anger. He saw Dixie and the doctor staring down at him and the Tucker children had stopped shouting and playing and were recoiling toward the walls.

"They *cannot* stay here!"

"But . . ."

"No!" Cudworth bellowed.

Dixie looked to Mrs. Cudworth and she thought the woman was going to wilt. "But, Mr. Cudworth, they are sick and in need of our help."

"I don't care! I want them removed."

Margaret Cudworth turned, hanging on to the balcony railing for support. Dixie had never seen such stricken eyes.

And even though she was disgusted by the poor woman's lack of gumption, she also felt a wave of pity.

Dr. Gentry cleared his throat. "I'm afraid that moving Reverend Tucker is out of the question, Mr. Cudworth."

Cudworth bristled. "Having a house full of dirty strangers is out of the question."

"Mr. Cudworth," Margaret cried. "Those are my *brother's* children. Your nephews and my nieces! They are *not* simply a bunch of 'dirty children' to be tossed out into our street like beggars."

"Mrs. Cudworth, how dare you speak to me so!" Roscoe Cudworth bellowed, stomping the floor in a rage.

"And how dare you insult my brother and his family!" Margaret screamed before she whirled and raced into the bedroom.

For a moment, Rosoe Cudworth was so stunned by his wife's uncharacteristic behavior that he could scarcely breath. He stood at the foot of the stairs puffing and looking outraged. He was a man in his late fifties and even from a distance, Dixie did not think he looked very well. He was too thin and his skin was the color of old parchment paper, wrinkled and a little yellow with jaundice. Despite his money, he looked like a miserable person.

"Sir," Dr. Gentry said, "you know that your heart is not strong. Getting all upset about this is not going to do your health any good at all. In fact, you look unwell."

Cudworth's hands flew to his hollowed cheeks. "I do?"

"Yes, you do," Gentry said, lowering his voice. "I can give you some heart medicine, but it won't help if you continue to become so upset about what is sure to be a temporary inconvenience."

Cudworth swallowed. "I don't even like *clean* children."

"These are part of your family, sir, and I guarantee they will clean up with a little soap and water."

"But they will wreck my solitude and destroy my . . . my tranquility!"

Gentry shook his head. He reached into his medical kit, removed a packet of powders, and descended the stairway, his voice smooth and reassuring. "Mr. Cudworth, your tranquility is very important, but how tranquil would life be if it became known in this town that you evicted your sick and destitute brother-in-law and his poor family?"

"What do you mean?"

Gentry looked up at Dixie and she swore that he winked at her. "I mean that the citizens of Austin might revolt in anger and withdraw their savings from your bank and refuse to buy from your mercantile."

"No!"

Gentry turned to look up at Dixie. "May I introduce Miss Dixie Ballou."

"Now who the hell is she!"

"I'm a friend of your brother-in-law and his family," Dixie said, her voice quaking with anger. "Me and my brother were the ones that amputated his leg out on the prairie while two Comanche helped hold him down!"

"Dear God," Cudworth gasped. "I need a drink."

"Miss Ballou's story will be very, very newsworthy," Gentry said. "I'm positive that our fine newspaper will make it front-page reading."

"Why!" Cudworth cried.

"Because it's an heroic story," the doctor explained. "And because it is also tragic and filled with drama. I wouldn't be surprised if the editor of the *Austin Daily Tribune* pays us a visit. But can you imagine the story he'd print if he discovers that you intend to toss this courageous family into the street?"

Apparently, Roscoe Cudworth could imagine, because

he staggered backward and his jaw dropped. "I need *two* drinks," he moaned.

"I could use one myself," the doctor said, "and we can talk about my fees in this matter and how even you can enhance your image and business tenfold by doing the right thing in this moment of family crisis."

Cudworth looked up at Dixie. He licked his lips nervously and then stared at the staring children. When the doctor joined him at the foot of the stairs, he hurried toward his parlor, where he no doubt had a liquor cabinet.

Dixie heard a door slam shut and then she turned and went into the bedroom to see Margaret Cudworth sobbing beside her sleeping brother.

"It's going to be all right," Dixie said, sitting down on the bed and placing a consoling hand on the poor woman's arm.

Margaret looked up at her. "But you don't know my husband."

"That's true," Dixie admitted, "but I'm already beginning to know Dr. Gentry, and he's going to make your husband see this in a much more charitable light than you might expect."

Margaret sniffled and wiped her eyes dry with her sleeve. "Do you really think so?"

"I do."

"Oh, I hope so!" the woman said with a passion. "He's become such an awful tyrant these last few years. It's as if money has become his personal god."

"It probably has," Dixie said, "but your brother will work a miracle on that kind of thinking."

"Poor Moody," she sighed. "He's had such a hard life. And now, with his leg missing, he can't even do any real work."

Dixie frowned. "That's just not true, Miss Cudworth. Your brother is a powerful preacher. I saw what he did in the town we left up in the Indian Territory. He was loved up there and highly respected."

"He was?"

"Yes."

Margaret brightened. "Did he ever say anything about his past?"

"Not to me," Dixie said, "but he told my brother that he'd once been a riverboat gambler on the Mississippi."

"And before that, a . . . a brothel bouncer!"

"Oh," Dixie said, feeling her cheeks warm. "Well, he's not the same man anymore. He's generous and filled with the love of our Lord. He has come to start up the Gospel Fire Church. And he also needs your help in buying a new printing press, ink, paper, and whatever other supplies that are required to print a church newspaper."

"Here in Austin!"

"Why not?" Dixie asked. "It was successful in Oklahoma and the Cherokee Indians up there are mostly a lot poorer than the people in Austin."

Margaret thought about that. "Well," she said, looking down at her brother, "we'll just see what happens. If my brother can get a single penny out of my husband, surely then, it will be an honest-to-God miracle."

SEVENTEEN

Dixie waited impatiently on the front porch until she saw Dr. Gentry come striding up the street, a happy whistle on his lips and a pleasant smile for everyone. As she watched the doctor, Dixie felt an unfamiliar stirring in her heart. It actually felt as if it had a flutter and Dixie noticed with some alarm the definite quickening of her pulse and wondered at her sudden nervousness.

What a handsome devil Dr. Gentry was! Also smart, intelligent, and sensitive. He had wavy brown hair and nice brown eyes. Perhaps his most appealing feature was his happy, generous mouth, and although he was not especially tall, neither was he short except by the standards of her father and brothers. Dixie wondered if the doctor was engaged to be married. He most certainly would have a sweetheart and Dixie would have bet that every single woman in Austin would be hot on his heels.

"Good morning, Miss Ballou!" he called, noticing her on the front porch. "What a difference a good night's sleep makes. You look like a new girl today! Bright and pretty as a daisy."

Dixie had taken a long bath and combed her black hair to a shine. She had borrowed a pretty yellow dress with white lace and proper shoes from Mrs. Cudworth. She had even squandered a few moments to admire herself in the mirror. But now, the word *girl* deflated her budding excitement.

"I'm not . . . a girl," she added lamely, realizing how petulant she sounded.

"I think you're a lovely girl," he said, stopping beside the porch and studying her with a broad smile. "Are you ready?"

"Of course."

"Then let's go and see what kind of a price we can get for those bone wagons and mules."

"It had better be a good one," Dixie said, "because I don't think that Mr. Cudworth is going to help the reverend and his family buy a printing press or anything else, for that matter."

The doctor offered Dixie his arm. She'd never taken one before but he kept the darn thing stuck out practically in her face until she slipped her arm through his. At that very instant, she realized that she'd made a mistake. Touching him made Dixie's pulse race even faster.

"The man I've talked to about buying the reverend's mules and wagons is named Abe Maxwell. Abe is our most successful horse trader and he'll try to beat us down to nothing. Figuring that in advance, I've also talked to another one of Austin's horse buyers and traders, a man named Joe Baylor. Baylor is rough and uncouth, but I know from personal experience that his word is his bond. If he makes an offer for the mules or the wagons, he'll stand by it and he pays cash."

"I won't give them away," Dixie said. "Mrs. Tucker really needs the money for her husband and all those children."

Gentry chuckled.

"What's so funny?"

"Charity," the doctor said, "is not in a horse trader's vocabulary. Neither one of these men cares if Mrs. Tucker's family is starving. They're both out to make a profit, pure and simple."

Dixie's first impulse was to say that she would not deal with such heartless men, but a moment's reflection made her realize that the doctor was right. Horse buying and selling was a business. What she had to offer was two pretty damn good teams of mules. As for the wagons and their cargos of bones, well, if the buyer didn't want the bones, he could dump them on the prairie. Both wagons were in good shape and their high sides could be easily removed if they proved to be bothersome.

When they arrived at the livery, Dixie went to the corral where she'd agreed to board the mules until they sold. The price was a dollar a day for the eight of them, and at that rate, Dixie knew that she could not afford to dicker around for several weeks. She was determined to unload the mules and the wagon this very morning if a fair price was offered.

"Good morning," a man said, coming over to meet them. He was in his fifties, a heavyset fellow with muttonchop whiskers and a fist-busted nose. He looked like an over-the-hill bare-knuckles brawler.

Dr. Gentry said, "Dixie, allow me to introduce Mr. Joe Baylor."

When they shook, Baylor's meaty fist engulfed Dixie's hand. He looked Dixie in the eye and said, "I've taken the liberty of already inspecting the two teams of mules and those bone wagons. How much do you want for them, cash on the barrelhead?"

"A hundred dollars for each team, harness and wagon," Dixie said, knowing that the price would have been a bargain back in Tennessee.

Baylor laughed out loud. "Ha, ha! Very funny, Miss Ballou. Very funny!"

The man's face stiffened and his eyes slitted. "Now, how much do you *really* want for everything?"

"A hundred dollars each," she repeated.

A pained expression came over Baylor's scarred face, "Now, Miss Ballou! A joke is a joke, but—"

"It's no joke."

"But I don't even want your bone wagons!"

"Then we have no further business to discuss, Mr. Baylor," Dixie said with a thin smile. "Good day."

"Doc!" the man groaned, looking to Gentry. "You've bought and sold a horse or two from me before, explain reality to this sweet girl."

"A hundred dollars for each outfit is perhaps a bit steep," the doctor opinioned.

"When is Mr. Maxwell coming?" Dixie asked.

Gentry consulted his pocket watch. "He should be here any moment."

"Then we'll see if he has any more charity in his heart."

"Charity!" Baylor exclaimed. "What has charity got to do with buying a bone wagon!"

Dixie explained to the man about the Reverend Tucker and his large family. "They intend to start a new church in Austin and they'll need some funds. Two hundred dollars won't be nearly enough, but it's the minimum."

"But I don't even go to church!"

"Then you should begin the moment that Reverend Tucker is physically able to conduct services," Dixie told the man. "You need to start acting like a generous Christian."

"Miss, I'm a horse trader! If I started trying to be a good Christian, I'd go broke. I'd starve!"

"With all due respect," Dixie said, her eyes dipping to the man's immense, sagging belly, "I don't think there's any danger of that."

Before Baylor could react, Dr. Gentry said, "Here comes Abe Maxwell."

"He won't give you near what I'll give you," Baylor snapped. "All right, my offer is seventy-five dollars cash for each outfit. That's the best I or anyone else in Austin would dare offer. Take it or leave it, Miss Ballou."

Dixie did not even dignify the offer with a response. Instead, she allowed the doctor to lead her forward to meet Abe Maxwell. He was also in his fifties, but outfitted in a well-tailored black suit with starched collar and white silk tie. His shoes were polished and two Negro boys about Dixie's age followed on his heels. They were dressed in white linen shirts and trousers and carried an armload of halters and lead ropes.

When the introductions had been made and before anyone could say a word, Joe Baylor quipped, "Abe, she wants a hundred dollars for each outfit. They're yours if you've been drinking again this morning."

Maxwell flushed with embarrassment. "What I have or have been doing is damn sure not your business, Joe. So why don't you run along and buy a burro or some chickens? That'll strain your finances, but—"

The two horse traders would have thrown themselves at each other right then and there except that Dr. Gentry managed to keep them separated. "Gentlemen!" he shouted. "We are professionals and this is business. Control yourselves!"

Maxwell jammed an expensive-looking cigar into the corner of his mouth. He snapped his fingers and one of his Negro boys jumped up and lit a match. "Joe, someday," Abe said, lips working around his cigar, "you're going to die and I'll have you dragged to the cemetery by jackasses."

"Ha!" Baylor shouted. "One of these days some horse is going to kick you in your big mouth and drive that fat Cuban cigar down your throat."

"Enough!" Gentry commanded. "Gentlemen, have you completely lost your senses! Apologize to this young lady at once!"

Both horse traders deflated. Joe Baylor jammed his fists

into his pockets and hum-hawed around for a few moments. He looked at Dixie, "I ahh. . . ."

"I've heard far worse, so forget it," Dixie said. "I'm just trying to get a fair price because the reverend and his family have no money and are forced to rely on the charity of Mr. Cudworth."

"Yeah," Baylor sympathized, "that's gotta be damn tough. And to show you that I do have charity in my heart, I'll give you ten percent over whatever cigar-face here is willin' to pay."

Maxwell exploded. "Oh, yeah! Well I'll give ten percent over that!"

"And I'll raise you ten!"

"Call!" Maxwell shouted.

"Gentlemen! So far we don't even have an offer to raise!" Gentry exclaimed.

"A hundred dollars for each wagon and team of mules is *my* offer," Maxwell proclaimed, glaring at Joe Baylor. "Match that!"

"One ten!"

"One twenty!"

"One . . . fifty!" Baylor shouted.

"Sold, you fat fool!" Maxwell crowed, pivoting on his heel and marching away, leaving the two Negro boys and a cloud of cigar smoke in his trail.

Baylor blinked and then he paled. It was obvious that he'd completely lost his senses and paid far too much money according to the local market for wagons and livestock.

Dixie almost felt sorry for the man but knew that he'd recoup his losses before very long. "I accept your offer of three hundred dollars for both wagons, teams, and harness, Mr. Baylor. And I want you to know that your generosity will not go unnoticed by the Lord because the money will be used by Reverend Tucker to spread the gospel."

Baylor moaned, "I hope he's watching, Miss Ballou. I hope he takes pity on me 'cause I'll lose my tail on this deal."

"Mr. Baylor," Gentry said, "remember, we are talking to a lady."

"Oh, yeah," the man said, looking a little green around the ears as he reached into his pocket and extracted a roll of Confederate currency.

"Union money only," Dixie said.

"But Texas is part of the Confederacy!"

"And everyone know that Confederate money is worthless," the doctor said. "And you know darn good and well that payment was understood to be in Union currency."

"But . . ."

"Union currency!" Gentry repeated, his voice taking on an edge. "Joe, if you don't make right on this, I swear that it'll ruin your good reputation in Austin."

For a moment, their eyes locked and just when Dixie was sure that Baylor was going to weasel out on the deal, the horse trader nodded. "All right, dammit! But she'll have to come to my bank. I don't carry around that kind of Yankee money."

The doctor consulted his pocket watch. "The banks are all open. Shall we?"

He gave Dixie his arm and she took it, feeling as happy as a sparrow in springtime. With Baylor shuffling dejectedly along behind, they headed up the street to the bank.

"How about a little lunch at the hotel to celebrate," Gentry said.

"I'd love it," Dixie replied, proud enough to bust the buttons on Mrs. Cudworth's borrowed blouse.

When the reverend and his wife learned of their good fortune to have three hundred dollars cash, they were ecstatic. "I'll hire a man to carve me some crutches," Tucker announced. "No, better yet, a wooden stump!"

"A stump?" his wife asked, looking shocked.

"Well, certainly. We'll go to a saddle maker and pay him to cut some straps and fasten the thing on and I'll get around better than ever."

"Mr. Tucker, maybe crutches would be more . . . well, appealing."

"Nonsense, Margaret! When I get to preaching, I can stomp my stump to emphasize my dramatic points! I'll have the children beat the thing up pretty good and it'll become a real asset. People will want to help me buy a new, laquered and shiny one. They'll take pity on this poor preacher. You'll see! The collection plate will come back to us overflowing."

"He might have something," Dixie told the woman.

Margaret didn't look too excited about the idea but she held her tongue. They sent for a carpenter and a saddle maker. Three days after that, they had Reverend Tucker stumping around in his bedroom waving his arms as he prepared his first Texas sermon and looking like some crazed Caribbean buccaneer.

When the reverend settled down, he asked Dixie to help him on one more small matter. "I need that printing press," he said. "And Mr. Cudworth absolutely refuses to help get my newspaper started. He won't consider helping even if I insert advertisements for his bank and mercantile."

"He's a hard man," Dixie said.

"Yes, but a fair one," Tucker said. "I just wish that he weren't so all-fired stingy! I've talked to him about how the Lord loves the giver until I'm blue in the face and it's as if he had a heart of stone."

"Maybe he'll change," Dixie said. "Maybe your coming here will be his salvation."

"That's what I've been hoping, too," the reverend said. "Mr. Cudworth isn't happy with all his money. He has indigestion and Margaret tells me he sleeps and eats poorly."

"Are you eating better?" Dixie asked.

"Like a horse," Tucker said, "and so are the rest of my family. Margaret says we gobbled up two months of her usual groceries in less than a week. She's worried sick about how to break the news to Mr. Cudworth."

"Margaret ought to tell the old skinflint off and be done with him," Dixie said.

"Oh, no!" Tucker replied. "Roscoe Cudworth may seem . . . well, a pagan, but I think he has the makings of a fine Christian. It's just going to take some work."

"You're the man that can do it."

"I don't think so," Tucker confessed. "He's got it in his mind that I'm . . . well, not much of a fella."

"That's not true," Anna said, coming into the room to take her husband's hand.

"It is true," Tucker argued. "He's a gifted businessman and has wealth. "I've got nothing and I come here as a freeloader."

"Stop it!" Anna said sternly. "Mr. Cudworth has never learned the grace of giving. He's got this big house, a bank, a mercantile, and ulcers. He doesn't know the meaning of the word *happiness* and not only has he made himself miserable, but he's made Margaret feel the same way."

"I don't know what to do," Tucker said, raising his hands and dropping them into his lap. "He's hardened his heart against me and won't listen to a word that I say. And he definitely won't help us to buy another printing press."

"The Lord will provide," Anna said.

Dixie listened but she had her own thoughts about Roscoe Cudworth and they were considerably less charitable. She excused herself and went downstairs and was leaving the house when she bumped into Dr. Gentry.

"Good morning!" he said. "Your expression tells me that you are filled with purpose."

Dixie smiled. "It does?"

"Yes. Your head was down and you had this intense look of concentration on your face as if you were locked into some difficult problem."

"I am," Dixie said, "but I think I have just figured out the solution."

"Want to tell me about it?"

Dixie shook her head. "I don't think so," she said. "But what is the name of your editor friend?"

"Jules Croft. Why?"

"No particular reason," Dixie said as she started to walk past.

"Whoa!" Gentry said. "Maybe I can help."

"If you did," Dixie told the doctor, "it might get you in a world of trouble."

"I'm not afraid to get into a little 'trouble' if the means justify the end."

"You mean that?"

"Yes."

"Then come along with me, Doctor. Because we are going to give Austin something to talk about for weeks."

Gentry gave her a curious look. Then he turned and studied the house. "I should check Mr. Tucker's bandages."

"They can wait another hour," Dixie said.

"Yes," Gentry mused aloud as he offered Dixie his arm. "I guess they can at that."

Three days later, the headlines of Austin's leading newspaper read:

CUDWORTH TURNS GOOD SAMARITAN!

News has just been received that Mr. Roscoe Cudworth, prominent Austin banker and mercantile owner has agreed to support his brother-in-law in his ministry as well as offering

Mr. Tucker a special role in his business.

Furthermore, Mr. Cudworth intends to tithe ten percent of his profits to Austin's worthiest charities. This could mean a tremendous boost to such good causes as the Ladies of the Civil War Society, the Stray Animal Welfare League, and the Reverend Tucker's new Gospel Fire Church. The idea, according to spokesperson Miss Dixie Ballou, is that Mr. Cudworth has decided to put the Lord first in his heart instead of the dollar.

Dixie and Dr. Gentry were standing just a few doors up the street when the newspaper opened its doors and copies were quickly distributed.

"I hope this doesn't backfire," the doctor said.

"What is there to lose?" Dixie asked. "If Cudworth refuses to go along with it, so what?"

"So he'll have you and your friends thrown out in the street."

"Do you really think he's going to be that foolish?" Dixie raised her finger and pointed. "Here they come."

And indeed, first one or two, then several more, and finally a complete delegation of Austin's citizens came marching down to Cudworth's Mercantile with newspapers in their hands.

"Let's slip in behind them and see what happens," Dixie said.

The doctor shook his head but he was grinning as he joined Dixie, and they fell in step with the crowd. When it reached Cudworth's Mercantile, they opened the door and filed inside.

"Roscoe!" the mayor shouted.

Roscoe Cudworth was working in the back storeroom. He appeared in the aisle, saw the huge crowd waiting and froze.

"Mayor, what's wrong!"

"Wrong? Why, absolutely nothing!" the mayor shouted. "We've come to congratulate you on your newfound generosity! What a wonderful gesture!"

Cudworth scuttled up the aisle. Dixie could see the look of wary confusion in the man's deep-set eyes. "What are you people talking about?"

"This!" the man said, slamming the newspaper down and turning it so that Cudworth could see his name in the headlines.

Cudworth's eyes bugged and his lower jaw dropped. He read the article very fast. "Why, I cannot . . ."

Mayor Tom Patterson slapped Cudworth on the back. "What a fine gesture! Roscoe, I can't speak for the others, but I confess that I never expected you to finally show this kind of civic responsibility."

"But . . ."

"And furthermore, I personally intend to start doing business here—on a regular basis."

"You will?"

"I will. I support businessmen who support Austin's needy citizens with their generosity. What we as businessmen take out of the community we must be willing to replenish, or the well will run dry."

The mayor turned the the crowd behind him. "Let's give three cheers for Mr. Cudworth!"

"Hip, hip, hooray! Hip, hip, hooray! Hip, hip, hooray!"

Dixie studied Cudworth's face. The skinflint was still in shock but he was actually grinning. Led by the mayor, people were pumping his hand and starting to move into his store looking for something to purchase.

"I told you old Roscoe was smart enough to figure out that generosity can pay," Dixie said.

"That's not why one should give," the doctor said. "Giving should be an unselfish act."

"I know that. You know that. Now, Roscoe Cudworth has finally learned as well."

The doctor laughed and took Dixie's arm. He led her back out into the street. "How old did you tell me you were?"

"Eighteen," she lied shamelessly.

Gentry chuckled. "You said fifteen and I'm afraid that I have to believe that, Miss Ballou."

"Does it make any difference?"

The doctor bent over, took her face in his hands, and kissed her forehead. "Yes, lovely girl."

"Damn," Dixie whispered as she took the doctor's arm.

They were nearing the corner of Congress Avenue and Second Street when a tall, slender horsemen on a big chestnut horse galloped past, causing Dixie to freeze in midstride.

"What's wrong?"

She relaxed. "For a moment, I thought that horseman was my brother. That's all."

"You're very, very fond of him, aren't you."

"Yes," Dixie said. "And that man reminds me very strongly of Rufus. He's very tall and sits a horse as if he were born to the saddle."

"I'd expect Rufus to return before too much longer."

"I hope so," Dixie said with a worried sigh. "With Houston maybe already dead up north . . . oh, my heavens!"

"What?"

"Ruff told me to check with the governor and find out if Houston had sent any letters from the North."

"He knows Governor Lubbock?"

"Of course not. But Houston didn't know where else to send word or have the news of his death forwarded. So he chose the governor's office."

The doctor shrugged. "That's perfectly logical. The governor's office is in the capitol building. We can walk there in five minutes."

When they arrived at the capitol building, they had little trouble finding the governor's office. A political aide told them that Governor Francis Lubbock was in San Antonio attending urgent meetings with leaders of the crumbling Confederacy.

"I have a brother named Houston Ballou," Dixie explained to the political aide. "He's loyal to the Confederacy and was going north to help a . . . a friend. Houston said he'd forward any mail he might have to this office."

"I see." The aide stared at Dixie so intently that the doctor snapped, "I'm a physician, young man. Are you having trouble with your eyes?"

"Oh, no, sir!"

"Then why don't you see if a letter from Houston Ballou has arrived?"

"It might be addressed to my brother Rufus Ballou," Dixie said quickly.

"I'll check," the aide said, scurrying up the hall.

After the young man had been gone for a few minutes, Dixie said, "You didn't need to snap at him like that."

"And he didn't need to gawk at you so."

"He wasn't gawking."

"He was."

"Well, I thought he was nice, and . . ."

"Here it is!" the aide said, waving a crumpled letter. "I keep them filed alphabetically, so your brother's letter was right in the front."

"Thank you," Dixie said, tearing it open.

The letter was very short. It read: "Dear Ruff and Dixie: Molly O'Day was murdered and I am locked up in a federal prison for the duration of this war. I hope someday to rejoin you in Texas. Do not worry, I will return. Love, your brother, Houston Ballou."

Dixie's eyes filled with tears and they spilled down her cheeks.

"Is he dead?" the aide asked.

"He's in prison," Dixie choked. "And the woman he loved, a southern spy, was murdered."

"I'm sorry," Gentry said, offering her his silk handkerchief. "I wish there was something I could say or . . . do."

Dixie steeled herself. Dried her eyes and raised her chin. "I just wish that Ruff was here, Dr. Gentry. I wish that his own life wasn't also in grave danger."

The doctor nodded with understanding and then he led Dixie out of the capitol building toward the Colorado River, where they took a long, quiet walk in the bright Texas sun.

EIGHTEEN

The Kiowa were camped about two miles north along the Witchita River and as the Comanche rode through the chill Texas predawn, Ruff could feel his insides turning to ice. From all indications, the Kiowa that had slaughtered the white couple and taken their small son was a large and well-armed hunting party. Even more troubling was the report from one of Buffalo Killer's scouts that the Kiowa had joined up with a half dozen whites who had ridden from the direction of Santa Fe. Buffalo Killer thought these white men to be Comancheros or slavers, men who would buy the white boy and any other captives that the Kiowa had taken during their lightning raid into east Texas.

"They will be hard fighters," Buffalo Killer warned. "And we must not let any escape."

Ruff had supposed that Buffalo Killer knew that these enemies, if allowed to escape, would bring grief and retribution to the Comanche villages. "How close will we get to them before we open fire?"

Buffalo Killer did not answer the question directly. Instead, he chose to look at High Fire and a smile touched the corners of his mouth.

"Horse very fast but not long runner, eh, Ruff?"

Ruff knew that he was being challenged to a horse race. What he did not understand was Buffalo Killer's timing.

"He'll run that pinto stallion of yours into the ground for a mile or two. The only reason you chased me down before was that my horse was already worn out."

Buffalo Killer shook his head. "Now we race to enemies for your rifle and knife."

Ruff barely managed to keep his jaw from dropping. "Are you proposing we race each other into the Kiowa camp?"

Buffalo Killer nodded.

"They'll hear us coming and shoot us out of our saddles!"

"You afraid?"

"Hell yes," Ruff admitted. "I was hoping to save the boy and return to Austin in one piece. Up until this very minute, it seemed like a reasonable enough plan."

"We ride first into battle, like Comanche warriors. We see which horse has the wings of the spirit wind. Comanche horse. Cherokee horse."

Ruff had the distinct impression that if he refused to race into the Kiowa camp he would lose all respect and probably die anyhow. The other Comanche were waiting for his answer and Ruff knew what it must be.

"We're going to get blown right out of the saddle, the both of us," he grumbled as he checked his weapons and leaned forward in his saddle.

High Fire felt Ruff's tension, and the stallion knew exactly what was about to happen. The Thoroughbred didn't understand why, because there were no racetrack crowds, no shrill cries from the bettors. But there was also no mistaking Ruff's tension, and when High Fire felt his reins lift and slacken, he leaped forward as Ruff's heels slapped his flanks.

The Thoroughbred was first to leap but Buffalo Killer's shorter-coupled pinto was quicker. Its powerful haunches and shoulders drove the Comanche warrior ahead of Ruff. The pinto laid its ears back and sailed across the prairie. Ruff ate huge clods of earth and he flattened down low on High

Fire and let the stallion settle into his long, fluid stride.

It took High Fire a quarter mile to overtake the sprinting pinto, and then they raced another half mile before High Fire's longer stride began to work to his advantage. Little by little, the Thoroughbred eased ahead as Ruff put his reins in his teeth and filled each fist with a loaded Colt .45.

The Kiowa camp loomed up suddenly. Ruff saw several small campfires and then a picket line of Indian ponies. He heard a shout of warning and then he saw the dark, moving silhouettes of scattering warriors. Ruff held his fire until High Fire was galloping past the Kiowa ponies. Buffalo Killer's pistol began to bang out from not far behind, and when someone up ahead leaped to his feet and howled, Ruff shot the warrior and then drove the stallion into the Kiowa camp.

The next few monents were unreal. Ruff emptied one pistol, hurled it away, and used a second, dropping both Kiowa and Comanchero. In the heat of the intense battle, Ruff suddenly felt High Fire shudder as the stallion took a bullet through the neck. The Thoroughbred faltered badly and before Ruff could draw it to a halt, the horse tumbled over an embankment and rolled down to the edge of the Witchita River.

"Oh, dammit!" Ruff cried, pulling himself to his feet and forgetting the great battle up above as he quickly examined the bullet wound. It took him only a moment to determine that the bullet had passed through the stallion's muscular neck without hitting an artery or the spine. Bleeding, however, was heavy.

"You're going to be fine," he told the suffering animal.

Ruff could hear the fierce battle raging up above and knew that he could not afford to stay and attend to his wounded horse, even if that meant it might bleed to death. If the Comanche lost this battle, then he wouldn't stand a chance of escape and he would have only himself to blame.

Yanking his bandanna from around his neck, Ruff tore it in half and then removed the stallion's bridle. He used the reins to tighten and hold his crude bandage against the twin bullet holes and hoped it would effectively stop the heavy bleeding.

A Kiowa's howl twisted Ruff about. He looked up to see a warrior leap off the embankment and attack with a knife. Ruff was out of bullets so he yanked his bowie knife free and hurtled forward. The Kiowa scored first. His knife burned fire across Ruff's ribs and they separated, each looking for an opening or some small advantage.

The Kiowa began to circle, trying to gain the higher ground while forcing Ruff to the river's edge. Ruff feinted a lunge and the Kiowa sprang backward. Realizing he'd been tricked, the warrior grinned and came in slashing, driving Ruff into the water.

The Kiowa looked very confident. He said something that had the unmistakable tone of contempt, and Ruff issued his own challenge: "Come on!"

The Kiowa attacked and instead of retreating deeper into the river, Ruff ducked under the Kiowa's flashing blade and kicked the Indian in the kneecap. The Kiowa staggered and Ruff was on the man, knife carving at his exposed ribs. The warrior grunted, tried to get his knife back into play, but Ruff slashed his forearm, and the Kiowa's knife spun into the river.

The Kiowa was bent over, left hand on his ribs, the right hand up high to ward off Ruff's next blow. Ruff could have finished him but instead did something totally unexpected. He smashed the unsuspecting Kiowa in the jaw with a sweeping uppercut. The warrior's eyes rolled upward and he crashed to the mud. Ruff stepped over him and tore his rifle from its scabbard, then scrambled up the embankment and into the small-scale Indian war. There was so much gun smoke that it took Ruff several moments to realize that the Comanche were finishing off the last of the Kiowa and Comancheros.

"Buffalo Killer!" Ruff yelled.

A warrior turned, saw Ruff, and hurled his knife. Ruff saw it as a mere blur of shining steel. He tried to twist out of its path, but it was too late and the knife sliced across his left shoulder. Ruff staggered, raised his Spencer rifle, and fired at the Kiowa. Only it wasn't a Kiowa, it was Long Bow, and he took the slug in the forehead and jerked over backward as if there were an invisible wire around his throat.

Ruff saw a Comanchero rise up behind Buffalo Killer. Being unarmed, he hurled his bowie knife at the white man. Knife throwing had never been Ruff's strong suit and it was no different now. The bowie's handle struck the Comanchero and knocked his aim off so that he shot wide.

Buffalo Killer whirled and shot the Comanchero. A few more scattered shots was followed by silence, quickly broken when Calling Hawk howled in victory. The fight was over and the Comanche warriors hurried off to claim the Kiowa ponies.

"Look," Buffalo Killer said, pointing to the trees.

Ruff saw a child lashed to a cottonwood tree. The boy was thin and had managed to scoot around behind the tree so that he was almost invisible from the Kiowa camp.

"Well, I'll be," Ruff said, sheathing his bowie and hurrying forward.

When Ruff knelt down beside the boy and cut him free, the kid stared at Ruff with fear in his eyes. Ruff tried to reassure him. "I know I look a sight," he said, "but I'm going to be fine and so are you, boy. What's your name?"

"Joel Kelly."

"How old are you?"

"Seven."

"You all right?"

The boy sniffled. He stared at Buffalo Killer. "Is he gonna scalp us now, mister?"

"No," Ruff said. "We're going away. We're going to Austin."

The boy nodded and his chin began to quiver. "They killed my ma and pa."

"I know," Ruff said. "We gave them a Christian burial. They're resting in peace now."

The boy took Ruff's hand and held it very tight.

The Comanche believed that the Kiowa camp was filled with evil spirits so they wanted to leave at once. They were happy and excited for they had captured many ponies.

"You keep tall horse," Buffalo Killer said. "You save my life."

"Are you sure?"

The Comanche chief nodded.

Ruff placed his hand on Buffalo Killer's shoulder. "You and your warriors are great Kiowa hunters."

The chief dipped his chin in agreement. Ruff collected High Fire's reins. The Thoroughbred stallion was weakened from blood loss and in obvious pain. His neck was held low and there was no way that Ruff would ride the horse. That was fine. Little Joel Kelly would ride him and Ruff was content to walk even though his slicked ribs and shoulder hurt like blazes.

Saying good-bye to the Comanche, with whom he'd rode, hunted, and fought, was not easy. In the short few weeks they'd been together, Ruff had formed a strong attachment to Buffalo Killer and most of his warriors.

"So long," he said. "Maybe we'll meet again someday, eh?"

"Maybe hunt buffalo and Kiowa, Ruff," Buffalo Killer said as he grabbed the mane of the pinto stallion and swung onto its back.

Ruff watched them gallop north, driving the Kiowa ponies and howling in victory. When they had vanished from his sight, he turned to the boy, gave him what he hoped was a reassuring smile, then led High Fire south, toward Austin.

It was a full day before Joel said, "What's this horse's name, mister?"

"High Fire."

"He's awful tall."

"Yep."

"Like you."

"Yep."

"Is he fast?"

Ruff twisted around and looked up at the kid. Joel Kelly was going to be all right—as all right as a boy could be who'd probably seen his parents impaled by Kiowa lances at age seven.

"Can he run, mister?"

Ruff stroked High Fire's muzzle and the Thoroughbred nuzzled his chest, wanting its ears to be scratched. Ruff obliged. He looked up and Joel was smiling.

Ruff smiled back, feeling pretty good about the way things had turned out. "Yeah, High Fire can run a little."

Joel stroked the stallion's muscular shoulder. "I bet he's faster than any old Indian pony!"

"Maybe old Roscoe Cudworth could use a boy to raise and help him spend all his money," Ruff mused aloud.

"Who's that, mister?"

"You'll meet him when we reach Austin," Ruff said. "And if he and his wife don't take an instant shine to you, I know a preacher and his good wife who will."

"A preacher?" The boy wasn't excited.

"Yeah," Ruff said, grinning easily to himself as he trudged south. "I sort of had the same poor reaction as you when I was first told I'd be hookin' up with a Bible thumper. But I grew to like him, Joel, and so will you."

"What's this preacher fella's name?"

"The Reverend Moody Tucker, and that's a name that's going to stand tall in Texas. Mark my word."

"I think I'd rather stay with you, mister."

"Well, Joel," Ruff said, "we'll have to wait and see how you get along with my sister and our Tennessee horses."

"Yes, sir! I like horses a lot but I don't know nothing about sisters!"

"Neither do I."

A mile later, Ruff glanced over his heavily bandaged shoulder and saw that Joel wore a faraway expression. Maybe he was thinking about horses, but Ruff also thought it might be that he was listening for the spirits of his dead parents. Maybe their spirits were flowing with the free wind across the Texas prairie, bidding their son good-bye and good luck.

That's how his Comanche friends would interpret Joel's expression, and for reasons Ruff did not fully understand, that made him feel even better.

I was hurt, though how badly I didn't know. Some three hours earlier I'd been shot, the ball taking me in the left side of the chest about midway up my rib cage. I didn't know if the slug had broken a rib or just passed between two of them as it exited my back. I'd been in Galveston, trying to collect a gambling debt, when, like a fool kid, I'd walked into a setup that I'd ordinarily have seen coming from the top of a tree stump. I was angry that I hadn't collected the debt, I was more than angry that I'd been shot, but I was furious at myself for having been suckered in such a fashion. I figured if it ever got around that Wilson Young had been gotten that easy, all of the old enemies I'd made through the years would start coming out of the woodwork to pick over the carcass.

But, in a way, I was lucky. By rights I should have been killed outright, facing three of them as I had and having nothing to put me on the alert. They'd had guns in their hands by the time I realized it wasn't money I was going to get but lead.

Now I was rattling along on a train an hour out of Galveston, headed for San Antonio. It had been lucky, me catching that train just as it was pulling out. Except for that, there was an excellent chance that I would have been incarcerated in Galveston and looking at more trouble than I'd been in in a long time. After the shooting I'd managed to get away from the office where the trouble had happened and make my way toward the depot. I'd been wearing a frock coat of a good quality linen when I'd sat down with Phil Sharp to discuss the money he owed me. Because it was a hot day, I took the coat off and laid it over the arm of the chair I was sitting in. When the shooting was over, I grabbed the coat and the little valise I was carrying and ducked and dodged my way through alleyways and side streets. I came up from the border on the train so, of course, I didn't have a horse with me.

But I did have a change of clothes, having expected to be overnight in Galveston. In an alley I took off my bloody shirt, inspected the wound in my chest, and then wrapped the shirt around me, hoping to keep the blood from showing. Then I put on a clean shirt that fortunately was dark and not white like the one I'd been shot in. After that I donned my frock coat, picked up my valise, and made my way to the train station. I did not know if the law was looking for me or not, but I waited until the train was ready to pull out before I boarded it. I had a round-trip ticket so there'd been no need for me to go inside the depot.

I knew I was bleeding, but I didn't know how long it would be before the blood seeped through my makeshift bandage and then through my shirt and finally showed on my coat.

All I knew was that I was hurting and hurting bad and that I was losing blood to the point where I was beginning to feel faint. It was a six-hour ride to San Antonio, and I was not at all sure I could last that long. Even if the blood didn't seep through enough to call it to someone's attention, I might well pass out. But I didn't have many options. There were few stops between Galveston and San Antonio, it being a kind of a spur line, and what there were would be small towns that most likely wouldn't even have a doctor. I could get off in one and lay up in a hotel until I got better, but that didn't much appeal to me. I wanted to know how bad I was hurt, and the only way I was going to know that was to hang on until I could get to some good medical attention in San Antone.

I was Wilson Young, and in that year of 1896, I was thirty-two years old. For fourteen of those years, beginning when I was not quite fifteen, I had been a robber. I'd robbed banks, I'd robbed money shipments, I'd robbed high-stakes poker games, I'd robbed rich people carrying more cash than they ought to have been, but mostly I'd robbed banks. But then about four years past, I'd left the owlhoot trail and set out to become a citizen that did not constantly have to be on the lookout for the law. Through the years I'd lost a lot of friends and a lot of members of what the newspapers had chosen to call my "gang"—the Texas Bank Robbing Gang in one headline.

I'd even lost a wife, a woman I'd taken out of a whorehouse in the very same town I was now fleeing from. But Marianne hadn't been a whore at heart; she'd just been kind of briefly and unwillingly forced into it in much the same way I'd taken up robbing banks.

I had been making progress in my attempt to achieve a certain amount of respectability. At first I'd set up on the Mexican side of the border, making occasional forays into Texas to sort of test the waters. Then, as a few years passed and certain amounts of money found their way into the proper hands, I was slowly able to make my way around Texas. I had not been given a pardon by the governor, but emissaries of his had indicated that the state of Texas was happy to have no further trouble with Wilson Young and that the past could be forgotten so long as I did nothing to revive it.

And now had come this trouble. The right or wrong of my position would have nothing to do with it. I was still Wilson

Young, and if I was in a place where guns were firing and men were being shot, the prevailing attitude was going to be that it was my doing.

So it wasn't only the wound that was troubling me greatly; it was also the worry about the aftermath of what had begun as a peaceful and lawful business trip. If I didn't die from my wound, there was every chance that I would become a wanted man again, and there would go the new life I had built for myself. And not only that life of peace and legality, but also a great deal of money that I had put into a business in Del Rio, Texas, right along the banks of the Rio Grande. Down there, a stone's throw from Mexico, I owned the most high-class saloon and gambling emporium and whorehouse as there was to be found in Texas. I had at first thought to put it on the Mexican side of the river, but the *mordida,* the bribes, that the officials would have taken convinced me to build it in Texas, where the local law was not quite so greedy. But now, if trouble were to come from this shooting, I'd have to be in Mexico, and my business would be in Texas. It might have been only a stone's throw away, but for me, it might just as well have been a thousand miles. And I'd sunk damn near every cent I had in the place.

My side was beginning to hurt worse with every mile. I supposed it was my wound, but the train was rattling around and swaying back and forth like it was running on crooked rails. I was in the last car before the caboose, and every time we rounded a curve, the car would rock back and forth like it was fixing to quit the tracks and take off across the prairie. Fortunately, the train wasn't very crowded and I had a seat to myself. I was sort of sitting in the middle of the double cushion and leaning to my right against the wall of the car. It seemed to make my side rest easier to stretch it out like that. My valise was at my feet, and with a little effort, I bent down and fumbled it open with my right hand. Since my wound had began to stiffen up, my left arm had become practically useless—to use it would almost put tears in my eyes.

I had a bottle of whiskey in my valise, and I fumbled it out and pulled the cork with my teeth and then had a hard pull. There was a spinsterish middle-aged lady sitting right across the aisle from me, and she give me such a look of disapproval that I thought for a second that she was going to call the conductor and make a commotion. As best I could, I got the cork back in the bottle and then hid it out of sight between my right side and the wall of the car.

Outside, the terrain was rolling past. It was the coastal prairie of south Texas, acres and acres of flat, rolling plains that grew the best grazing grass in the state. It would stay that way until the train switched tracks and turned west for San Antonio. But that was another two hours away. My plan was to get myself fixed up in San Antone and then head out for Del Rio and the Mexican side of the border just as fast as I could. From there I'd try and find out just what sort of trouble I was in.

That was, if I lived that long.

With my right hand I pulled back the left side of my coat, lifting it gently, and looked underneath. I could see just the beginning of a stain on the dark blue shirt I'd changed into. Soon it would soak through my coat and someone would notice it. I had a handkerchief in my pocket, and I got that out and slipped it inside my shirt, just under the stain. I had no way of holding it there, but so long as I kept still, it would stay in place.

Of course I didn't know what was happening at my back. For all I knew the blood had already seeped through and stained my coat. That was all right so long as my back was against the seat, but it would be obvious as soon as I got up. I just had to hope there would be no interested people once I got to San Antone and tried to find a doctor.

I knew the bullet had come out my back. I knew it because I'd felt around and located the exit hole while I'd been hiding in the alley, using one shirt for a bandage and the other for a sop. Of course the hole in my back was bigger than the entrance hole the bullet had made. It was always that way, especially if a bullet hit something hard like a bone and went to tumbling or flattened out. I could have stuck my thumb in the hole in my back.

About the only good thing I could find to feel hopeful about was the angle of the shot. The bullet had gone in very near the bottom of my ribs and about six inches from my left side. But it had come out about only three or four inches from my side. That meant there was a pretty good chance that it had missed most of the vital stuff and such that a body has got inside itself. I knew it hadn't nicked my lungs because I was breathing fine. But there is a whole bunch of other stuff inside a man that a bullet ain't going to do a bit of good. I figured it had cracked a rib for sure because it hurt to breathe deep, but that didn't even necessarily have to be so. It was hurting so bad anyway that I near about couldn't separate the different kinds of hurt.

And a more unlikely man than Phil Sharp to give me my seventh gunshot wound I could not have imagined. I had ended my career on the owlhoot trail with my body having lived through six gunshots. That, as far as I was concerned, had been a-plenty. By rights I should have been dead, and there had been times when I had been given up for dead. But once off the outlaw path I'd thought my days of having my blood spilt were over. Six was enough.

And then Phil Sharp had given me my seventh. As a gambler I didn't like the number. There was nothing lucky about it that I could see, and I figured that anything that wasn't lucky had to be unlucky.

Part of my bad luck was because I *was* Wilson Young. Even though I'd been retired for several years, I was still, strictly speaking, a wanted man. And if anybody had cause to take interest in my condition, it might mean law—and law would mean trouble.

For that matter Phil Sharp and the three men he'd had with him might have thought they could shoot me without fear of a murder charge because of the very fact of my past and my uncertain position with regard to the law, both local and through the state. Hell, for all I knew some of those rewards that had been posted on my head might still be lying around waiting for someone to claim them. It hadn't been so many years past that my name and my likeness had been on Wanted posters in every sheriff's office in every county in Texas.

I had gone to see Phil Sharp because he'd left my gambling house owing me better than twenty thousand dollars. I didn't, as an ordinary matter, advance credit at the gaming tables, but Sharp had been a good customer in the past and I knew him to be a well-to-do man. He owned a string of warehouses along the docks in Galveston, which was the biggest port in Texas. The debt had been about a month old when I decided to go and see him. When he'd left Del Rio, he'd promised to wire me the money as soon as he was home, but it had never come. Letters and telegrams jogging his memory had done no good, so I'd decided to call on him in person. It wasn't just the twenty thousand; there was also the matter that it ain't good policy for a man running a casino and cathouse to let word get around that he's careless about money owed him. And in that respect I was still the Wilson Young it was best not to get too chancy with. Sharp knew my reputation and I did not figure to have any trouble with him. If he didn't have the twenty thousand handy, I figured we could come to some sort of agreement as to how he could pay it off. I had wired him before I left Del Rio that I was planning a trip to Houston and was going to look in on him in Galveston. He'd wired back that he'd be expecting me.

I saw him in his office in the front of one of the warehouses he owned down along the waterfront. He was behind his desk when I was shown in, getting up to shake hands with me. He was dressed like he usually was, in an expensive suit with a shiny vest and a big silk tie. Sharp himself was a little round man in his forties with a kind of baby face and a look that promised you could trust him with your virgin sister. Except I'd seen him without the suit and vest, chasing one of my girls down the hall at four o'clock in the morning with a bottle of whiskey in one hand and the handle to his hoe in the other. I'd also seen him at the poker table with sweat pouring off his face as he tried to make a straight beat a full house. It hadn't then and it probably never would.

He acted all surprised that I hadn't gotten my money, claiming he'd mailed it to me no less than a week ago. He said, "I got to apologize for the delay, but I had to use most of my ready cash on some shipments to England. Just let me step in the next room and look at my canceled checks. I'd almost swear I saw it just the other day. Endorsed by you."

Like I said, he looked like a man that might shoot you full of holes in a business deal, but not the sort of man who could use or would use a gun.

He got up from his desk and went to a door at the back, just to my right. I took off my coat and laid it over the arm of the chair, it being warm in the office I was sitting kind of forward on the chair, feeling a little uneasy for some reason. It was that, but it was mainly the way Sharp opened the back door that probably saved my life. When you're going through a door, you pull it to you and step to your left, toward the opening, so as to pass through. But Sharp pulled open the door and then stepped back. In that instant, I slid out of the chair I was sitting in and down to my knees. As I did, three men with hoods pulled over their heads came through the door with pistols in their hands. Their first volley would have killed me if I'd still been sitting in the chair. But they fired at where I'd been, and by the time they could cock their pistols for another round, I had my revolver in my hand and was firing. They never got off another shot; all three went down under my rapid-fire volley.

Then I became aware that Phil Sharp was still in the room, just by the open door. I was about to swing my revolver around on him when I saw a little gun in his hand. He fired, once, and hit me in the chest. I knew it was a low-caliber gun because the blow of the slug just twitched at my side, not even knocking me off balance.

But it surprised me so that it gave Sharp time to cut through the open door and disappear into the blackness of the warehouse. I fired one shot after him, knowing it was in vain, and then pulled the trigger on an empty chamber.

I had not brought any extra cartridges with me. In the second I stood there with an empty gun, I couldn't remember why I hadn't brought any extras, but the fact was that I was standing there, wounded, with what amounted to a useless piece of iron in my fist. As quick as I could, expecting people to suddenly come bursting in the door, I got over to where the three men were laying on the floor and began to check their pistols to see if they fired the same caliber ammunition I did. But I was out of luck. My revolver took a .40-caliber shell; all three of the hooded men were carrying .44-caliber pistols.

Two of the men were dead, but one of them was still alive. I didn't have time to mess with him, but I turned him over so he could hear me good and said, "Tell Phil Sharp I ain't through with him. Nor your bunch either."

Then I got out of there and started making my way for the train depot. At first the wound bothered me hardly at all. In fact I at first thought I'd just been grazed. But then, once outside, I saw the blood spreading all over the front of my shirt and I knew that I was indeed hit. I figured I'd been shot by nothing heavier than a .32-caliber revolver but a .32 can kill you just as quick as a cannon if it hits you in the right place.

857